"I need you to be careful." He was so solemn, so serious.

Her throat constricted and her heart beat so hard she was sure her whole body vibrated from the violence of it.

His grip on her chin softened, his fingertip moving along the line of her jaw. She wanted to melt into a puddle, but she wasn't seventeen anymore, and with that frisson of delight she was reminded she *hated* Ty Carson.

She slapped his hand away, raising her chin at him, trying for regal instead of panicked. "Don't manhandle me."

He only raised an eyebrow.

"I don't know what you want from me," she said, with more feeling than she should have shown him.

"I want you to be aware. Take precautions. Keep yourself safe and protected." He moved out of the way of the door and her exit. "It's that simple."

Simple? Sure. As if anything to do with Ty Carson was *simple*.

WYOMING COWBOY RANGER

NICOLE HELM

For anyone who found the courage to go home again,
and those who had the bravery to stay.

ISBN-13: 978-1-335-64089-5

Wyoming Cowboy Ranger

This edition published by arrangement with Harlequin Books S.A.

For questions and comments about the quality of this book, please contact us at CustomerService@Harlequin.com.

Printed in U.S.A.

Nicole Helm grew up with her nose in a book and the dream of one day becoming a writer. Luckily, after a few failed career choices, she gets to follow that dream—writing down-to-earth contemporary romance and romantic suspense. From farmers to cowboys, Midwest to *the* West, Nicole writes stories about people finding themselves and finding love in the process. She lives in Missouri with her husband and two sons and dreams of someday owning a barn.

Books by Nicole Helm

Harlequin Intrigue

Carsons & Delaneys: Battle Tested

Wyoming Cowboy Marine
Wyoming Cowboy Sniper
Wyoming Cowboy Ranger

Carsons & Delaneys

Wyoming Cowboy Justice
Wyoming Cowboy Protection
Wyoming Christmas Ransom

Stone Cold Texas Ranger
Stone Cold Undercover Agent
Stone Cold Christmas Ranger

Harlequin Superromance

A Farmers' Market Story

All I Have
All I Am
All I Want

Falling for the New Guy
Too Friendly to Date
Too Close to Resist

Visit the Author Profile page at Harlequin.com.

CAST OF CHARACTERS

Tyler "Ty" Carson—Former army ranger. He's now home in Bent, Wyoming, for good, but is receiving letters threatening his family and his first love, Jen Delaney.

Jen Delaney—Ty's secret high school sweetheart. Runs the Delaney General Store in Bent. She was heartbroken when Ty left town without a word, so she's determined to avoid him as much as possible. Members of their families marrying each other is making it difficult. She thinks Ty is paranoid about her being in danger, until she starts to receive unnerving visits from a stranger.

Thomas Hart—A sheriff's deputy with the Bent County sheriff's department. Dated Jen a few times.

Braxton Lynn—The writer of the threatening letters to Ty. No one can figure out what connection he has to Ty or Jen.

Zach Simmons—Ty's cousin, whom he's only recently learned about, and a former FBI agent working for Jen's brother. He helps Ty and Jen with some security measures.

Laurel Delaney-Carson—Jen's sister and a detective with the sheriff's department. She's on desk duty due to pregnancy.

Grady Carson—Ty's cousin and Laurel's husband. Grady runs Rightful Claim, Bent's saloon—where Ty lives in the apartment above.

Chapter One

Jen Delaney loved Bent, Wyoming, the town she'd been born in, grown up in. She was a respected member of the community, in part because she ran the only store that sold groceries and other essentials within a twenty-mile radius of town.

From her position crouched on the linoleum while she stocked shelves, she looked around the small town store she'd taken over at the ripe age of eighteen. For the past ten years it had been her baby with its narrow aisles and hodgepodge of necessities.

She'd always known she'd spend the entirety of her life happily ensconced in Bent and her store, no matter what happened around her.

The reappearance of Ty Carson didn't change that knowledge so much as make it…annoying. No, annoying would have been just his being in town again. The fact their families had somehow intermingled in the last year was… a catastrophe.

Her sister, Laurel, marrying Ty's cousin Grady had been a shock, very close to a betrayal, though it was hard to hold it against Laurel when Grady was so head over heels for her it was comical. They both glowed with love and happiness and impending parenthood.

Jen tried not to hate them for it.

She could forgive Cam, her oldest brother, for his serious relationship with Hilly. Hilly was biologically a Carson, but she'd only just found that out. Besides, Hilly wasn't like other Carsons. She was so sweet and earnest.

But Dylan and Vanessa… Her business-minded, sophisticated older brother *impregnating* and marrying snarky bad girl Vanessa Carson… *That* was a nightmare.

And none of it was fair. Jen was now, out of nowhere, surrounded by Carsons and Delaneys intermingling—which went against everything Bent had ever stood for. Carsons and Delaneys hated each other. They didn't fall in love and get married and have *babies*.

And still, she could have handled all that in a certain amount of stride if it weren't for *Ty* Carson. Everywhere she turned he seemed to be right there, his stoic gaze always locked on *her*, reminding her of a past she'd spent a lot of time trying to bury and forget.

When she'd been seventeen and the stupidest girl alive, she would have done anything for Ty Carson. Risked the Delaney-Carson curse that, even with all these Carson-Delaney marriages, Bent still had their heart set on. She would have risked her father's wrath over daring to connect herself with a *Carson*. She would have given up anything and everything for Ty.

Instead he'd made promises to love her forever, then disappeared to join the army—which she'd found out only a good month after the fact. He hadn't just broken her heart—he'd crushed it to bits.

But Ty was a blip of her past she'd been able to forget about, mostly, for the past ten years. She'd accepted his choices and moved on with her life. For a decade she had grown into the adult who didn't care at all about Ty Carson.

Then Ty had come home for good, and all she'd convinced herself of faded away.

She was half convinced he'd returned simply to make her miserable.

"You look angry. Must be thinking about me."

Her head whipped up, the jolt of surprise having nothing on the white-hot flash of fury. "I never think about you, Tyler." She definitely wasn't about to admit she *had* been.

His cocksure grin faded somewhat. He hated his full first name with a passion she'd certainly never understood, but it was one of the few tools in her arsenal she had to get under his unflappable demeanor.

He wasn't the only person who made her want to lash out, but considering what he'd done to her, she didn't make an effort to curb that impulse like she did with everyone else.

She slowly rose from where she'd been crouched, dusting her hands off by slapping them together. "Don't you have anything better to do than stalk me?" she asked haughtily, sailing past him in the narrow aisle with as much grace as she could muster.

"Don't flatter yourself, babe."

Babe. Oh, she'd like to knock his teeth out. Instead she scooted behind the checkout counter and smiled sweetly at him. "Then might I kindly suggest you make your purchases."

"You really think I'd be talking to you if I didn't have to be? I've got ample time to corner you if I wanted to at a family gathering with all the recent Carson-Delaney insanity going around."

She narrowed her eyes at him. He'd always been tall, rangy, dangerous. Age only enhanced all of those things. It was hardly fair he looked even better now than he had then. Certainly unfair he was talking to her as if *she'd* been the one to disappear in the middle of the night a decade ago.

"So what is it you want?" she demanded, but the fact he had a point had fear sneaking past her Ty-defenses. "There's not more trouble, is there?" Bent had been a beacon for it lately.

Laurel and Dylan and even Vanessa dang Carson might be going around town yapping they didn't believe in curses or love solved curses or *whatever*, but trouble after trouble didn't lie. Jen was convinced there had to be *something* to the old curse that said a Carson and Delaney falling in love only spelled trouble.

"No trouble," Ty said casually. "Just a concern. We'll call it a gut feeling."

Develop those off army rangering, did you? She bit her tongue so the words wouldn't escape and reveal how many scraps of information she'd collected about him over the years.

"How can *I* help?" *Mr. Army Ranger should take care of his gut feelings himself, shouldn't he?*

"I just need you to give me a heads-up if you get any new people in the store. You can even send the info through Hilly or Addie, if you'd rather."

Jen raised her chin. It'd be a cold day in hell before she gave this heartless, careless jerk any clue she still had feelings for him. "I don't need to go through anyone, but surely you don't need to know every single stranger I get in here."

"And just how many strangers do you typically get in here?" Ty asked drily.

"Enough."

He didn't respond right away, though she could tell by the tiniest firming of his mouth that he was irritated with her. It nearly made her smile. Ty was not an easy man to irritate—at least not visibly.

"This isn't about us," he said in low, heavy tones.

Any twitch of a smile died. *Us.* They did not acknowledge *us*, and hadn't since his return. There'd been no mention that they'd ever sworn their love for each other. They'd been stupid teenagers, yes, but she'd so believed those words.

"We've had enough trouble lately," Ty said, and she hated that she could see the stiffness in his posture. Anyone else wouldn't have noticed the change, but she knew him too well even all these years later to miss that slight tightening in the way he held himself. "If there's going to be more, I want to head it off at the pass. You run the most visited place in Bent. All I'm asking is for you to—"

"Yes, I understand what you're asking," she replied primly. "Consider it done. Now, feel free to leave." Because she hated him here. Hated breathing the same air as him. Hated looking into those blue eyes she knew too well, because his build could change, the skin around his eyes could crinkle with the years, but the sharp blue of tropical ocean would always be the exact same.

And it would always hurt, no matter how much she tried to exorcise that pain.

He rapped his knuckles against her counter lightly, his lips curved into something like a wry smile. "See you around, Jen."

Not if I can help it.

TY COULDN'T EXPLAIN the feeling that needled along his spine. It had nothing to do with the heavy weight that settled in his stomach. The needling was his gut feeling, honed as an army ranger, that told him the strange, threatening letters he'd been receiving weren't a prank or a joke.

The hard ball of weight was all Jen. Regrets. Guilt. Things he'd never, ever expected to feel, but adulthood had changed him. The army and army rangers had changed him. All the regrets he swore to himself at eighteen to never, ever entertain swamped him every time he saw her.

He tried not to see her, but his family was making it even harder than this small town.

All that was emotional crap he could at least pretend to ignore or will away. Which was exactly what he could not do with the latest letter that had been mixed in with the other mail to Rightful Claim, the bar his cousin owned and where Ty worked.

Vague. Ominous. Unsigned. And addressed to him. He had his share of enemies in Bent. Being a Carson in this town lent itself toward Delaney enemies everywhere he went. But though he'd love to pin it on a Delaney or a crony of theirs, it wasn't.

This was something outside, which meant it likely connected to his time in the army. Yeah, he'd made a few enemies there, too. He wasn't a guy who went looking for trouble. In fact, he could get along with just about anyone.

Until he couldn't.

He blew out a breath as he crossed Main. Away from the prim and tidy Delaney side of the street, to the right side. The rough-and-tumble Carson side with Rightful Claim at the end—with its bright neon signs and assurance that nothing in this town would ever be truly civilized like the Delaneys over there wanted.

Except the lines weren't so clear anymore, were they?

Dylan Delaney was standing in the garage opening to Carson Cars & Bikes. Vanessa and her swell of a baby bump stood next to him, grinning happily up at the man she used to hate.

What was *wrong* with his cousins? He could give a pass to his brother. Noah's wife was barely a Delaney. Oh, somewhere along the line, but Addie hadn't grown up here. Dylan and Laurel? Born and bred rule-abiding proper Delaney citizens, and somehow Vanessa and Grady were head over heels in dumb.

Ty should know, shouldn't he? He'd been there first. He'd just had the good sense to get the hell out of that mess while he could.

But that only conjured images of Jen, who hadn't had the decency to change in his near decade away. Once upon a time he'd been stupid enough to count the freckles on her nose and commit that number to memory.

It wasn't the first time he wished he could medically remove the part of his brain still so in tune to that long past time, and it probably wouldn't be the last.

He didn't nod or greet Dylan as he passed and felt only moderately guilty for being rude. Until Vanessa's voice cut through the air.

"Hey, jerkoff."

He heaved out a sigh and slowly turned to face her. Her baby bump was so incongruous to the sharp rest of her. "Yes, Mrs. Delaney," he replied.

She didn't even flinch, just slid her arm around Dylan's waist. As though a Carson and a Delaney—opposites in every possible way—could be the kind of lifetime partners real marriages were made out of.

If he could erase four years of his adolescent life, it would have been funny. He would have had a heck of a time making fun of all of the fallen Carsons. But since he'd given all *that* up once upon a time, and no one had any clue, all this wedded bliss and the popping out of babies was hard to swallow.

"You coming to the baby shower?" Vanessa demanded. Marriage and pregnancy hadn't softened her any. At least there was that.

"Do I look like the kind of man who goes to baby showers?"

"Oh, don't be a wuss. It's coed."

"It's co-no."

"Noah's coming."

Hell.

"You're way more of a baby shower guy than Noah."

"I take offense to that."

She grinned. "Good. I'll count you down for a yes."

"I don't think—"

"Give him a break, Van," Dylan said, his arm resting across her shoulders, as if just a few months ago they hadn't hated each other's guts. "It's only because Jen's going to be there."

Ty stiffened, fixing Dylan with an icy look. "What's Jen got to do with anything?"

Vanessa's smile went sly, but she nodded agreeably to her husband's words. "It's no secret you two *hate* each other." She enunciated the word *hate* as if it didn't mean what it ought.

But it darn well had to. "I can't stand the whole lot of you, but I've suffered through a few weddings now—a lot better than the two of you did on that first one," he replied, nodding toward Vanessa's expanding stomach.

Vanessa rubbed her belly. "That was fate."

"That was alcohol. Now, I have things to do."

"One o'clock tomorrow. Don't be late."

He grunted. He could disappear for the night, easily enough. Even his brother wouldn't be able to find him. But Noah would be disappointed if he baled. Worse, Noah's wife, Addie, would be disappointed in him. She'd give him that wounded deer look.

Damn Delaney females.

Ty stalked down the street, edgy and snarling

and with nothing to take it out on. He pushed into Rightful Claim knowing he had to rein in his temper lest Grady poke at it. Though Grady owned Rightful Claim, Ty lived above it and worked most nights as a bartender.

He'd been toying around with the idea of convincing Grady to let him buy in as partner. He just wasn't 100 percent sure he wanted to be home for good. He was done with the army rangers, that much was for sure, but that didn't mean he was ready to water the roots that tied him to Bent.

Didn't mean he wasn't. The problem was he wasn't sure. Until he was, he was going to focus on taking it one day at a time.

Grady looked up from his place behind the bar where he was filling the cash register to get it ready for the three o'clock opening. "You got a letter in the mail," Grady offered lightly, nodding toward a pile of envelopes and glossy postcards. "No postage. Odd."

Ty shrugged and snatched up the letter with his name on it. "Women never leave you secret admirer notes, Grady?"

"No, women used to leave me themselves," Grady said with a sharp grin.

"Used to," Ty replied with a snort. "Old married man."

"Ain't half-bad with the right marriage, in my experience."

"Sage advice from the married-for-less-than-a-year. You come talk to me when you've got a few decades under your belt."

"Won't change anything," Grady replied with a certainty that didn't make any sense to Ty. How could anyone possibly be sure? Especially Grady? His mother had been married more times than Ty could count. At least Ty's dad had had the good sense to stop after Mom had died. Focused his making people miserable on his kids instead of on a new woman.

"You okay?" Grady asked casually enough.

"Why wouldn't I be okay?"

"You seem…"

Ty looked up at his cousin and raised an eyebrow.

"Edgy," Grady finished, heeding none of Ty's nonverbal warnings.

"I'm always edgy," Ty said, trying to flash the kind of grin he always flashed. It fell flat, and he knew it.

"No. You're always a little sharp, a little hard, but you're not usually *edgy*."

Ty shrugged. "Just waiting for the curse to hit us trifold. Or is it quadruple-fold? Can't keep up with you all."

"If you believe in town curses, it's out-of-your-mind-fold." Grady still stood behind the cash register even though he'd finished his work. "If you've got trouble, you only need to share it, cousin. Mine, cow or woman?"

Ty wanted to smile at the old code they'd developed as kids. But the problem was he didn't know *what* kind of trouble he'd brought home. Whatever trouble it was, though, it was his problem. They'd had enough around here lately, and with Van and Laurel pregnant, Ty wasn't going to make a deal about things.

He was going to handle it. He always handled it.

"Be down for opening," Ty grumbled, dreading the Saturday night crowd. He moved through the bar to the back room, not looking down at the letter clutched in his fist. He walked up the stairs, forcing himself not to break into a jog. When he stepped into his apartment, he ripped open the envelope, trying not to focus on the lack of postage.

He pulled out a small, white piece of paper, eyes hurrying over the neatly printed words.

It must be nice to be home with the people you love—family, sure, but first loves most of all.

It won't be so nice to lose. One or the other.

Ty crumpled the note as his hand curled into a fist. He reared his arm back, ready to hurl it into the trash, but he stopped himself.

He smoothed the note out on the counter and studied it. Whoever was threatening him anonymously would have to be stopped.

Which meant he had to figure out who wanted to hurt him and was close enough to drop an unstamped letter in his mailbox.

The people you love.

Not on his watch.

JEN DELANEY WAS as pretty as he'd been told. It gave him a little thrill. As did watching her while she hadn't a clue anyone was watching. She stocked shelves, waited on the occasional customer, all while he watched from the viewfinder of his camera.

He'd had to take a break when Ty Carson had sauntered up, but that had given him time to leave the note.

Ty Carson.

Feeling the black anger bubble in his gut, he lowered the camera. He took deep calming breaths, and counted backward from ten just like Dr. Michaels always told him to.

He found his calm. He found his purpose. He slid into the car he'd parked in the little church parking lot. He exchanged his camera for his binoculars.

He could just barely make Jen out through

the storefront of Delaney General. She was the perfect target. In every way.

And when he targeted her, he'd make Ty fear. He'd make Ty hurt. He'd ruin his life, step by step.

Just like Ty had ruined his.

On one last breath, he smiled at himself in the rearview mirror. Calm and happy, because he had his plan in place.

Step one: charm Jen Delaney.

It shouldn't be hard. He knew everything about her. Thanks to Ty.

Chapter Two

Saturday evenings at Delaney General were always fairly busy. During the week Jen's crowd was minimal and usually the browsing kind. Weekends were more frantic—trips to grab what had been forgotten over the week. A twelve-pack of beer, sauce for spaghetti already on the stove and, in the case of one nervous young gentleman, a box of condoms.

She'd made one joke about telling his mother. He'd scurried away, beet red. There was *some* joy in living in a small town. Jim Bufford hefted a twenty-four-pack of her cheapest beer onto the checkout counter and grinned at her, flashing his missing bottom tooth. "Care to drink dinner with me, darling?"

"Hmm," she replied, pulling the case over the scanner. Jim had been making this particular offer since she'd turned twenty. Since he made it to just about every female who'd ever worked in Delaney General, she didn't take it personally. "Some other night, Jim. Got my nose to the grindstone here."

He handed over a wad of wrinkled bills and tutted while she made change. "Young pretty thing shouldn't work so hard."

"And a nice man like you shouldn't drink his dinner." She handed him his change and he hefted the case off the counter.

"Yeah, yeah," he grumbled, offering a half-hearted goodbye as he pushed open the door and stepped out. Just a few seconds later the bell on the door tinkled again and someone stepped inside.

She didn't recognize this customer. He wore his cowboy hat low, obscuring most of his face. Still, she could usually recognize her regulars by size, clothes, posture and so on. This was a stranger.

She remembered Ty's words from earlier and an icy dread skittered up her spine, but she smiled. "Good evening."

"Evening," the man returned, a pleasant smile of his own. She couldn't see his eyes, but his smile wasn't off-putting. He was wearing what appeared to be hiking gear and had a fancy-looking camera hanging from his neck. "I don't suppose you carry film?" He lifted the camera and his smile turned sheepish.

"Afraid not."

He sighed. "Didn't expect to use so much. You've got a fascinating town here, ma'am."

"We like to think so." She kept her smile in place. The man was perfectly polite. No different from any other stranger who walked into her store looking for provisions of any kind.

Her palms were sweaty, though, and her heart beat too hard. It was only her and him in the store right now, and Ty had warned her about strangers.

And you're going to trust Ty Carson on anything? No. No, she wasn't, but… Well, there'd been too much trouble lately not to heed his warning. So, she'd be smart. Do what her deputy sister would do in this situation: pay attention to details. The man was tall, maybe around her brother Cam's height. But not broad. He had narrow shoulders, though the way he walked exuded a kind of strength. Like a runner, she supposed. Slim, but athletic. She couldn't determine the exact shade of his hair because of the way the hat was positioned and the way he was angled away from her, but it wasn't dark hair.

"I don't have film, but I've got food and drinks or anything else you might need." She smiled at him, but he still didn't look her way. He examined the store.

"Actually I stopped because I was wondering if you'd mind if I took a few pictures of your store."

"I thought you were out of film."

"I am, which is a shame. But I use my phone for pictures, too. I was using film out here because the ambiance seemed to call for it. I was over at the saloon. I hear the swinging doors are original."

"So they claim," Jen muttered, irritably thinking of Ty.

"Amazing." He meandered over to a row of candy, studied the offerings. "I took way too many pictures. And the boardwalks. The signs. It's like stepping back in time. I've been mostly sticking to ghost towns but the mix of past and present here… It's irresistible."

"So you were out at Cain, then?" she asked, referencing a popular ghost town destination for photographers and adventurers.

He nodded, still keeping his head tilted away from her. "That's what brought me out this way."

"From where?"

He chuckled. "You ask every stranger where they're from?"

She had to work to keep the pleasant smile on her face. She couldn't blow this. "Tend to. We don't get many outsiders."

"Ah. Outsiders. Must be nice to live in a

community that protects itself against outsiders. You'd feel…safe. Protected and cared for."

She hadn't felt particularly safe after the craziness of the past year, but she decided to agree anyway. "Very."

He swayed on his feet, trying to brace himself on the shelf and upending some candy before he fell backward onto the floor.

Stunned, Jen rushed forward, but he was already struggling to sit up.

"I'm all right," he said, holding out a hand to keep her back. "Just haven't eaten since breakfast. Got caught up, and I suppose the lack of food caught up with me. I'll be all right."

She grabbed one of the candy bars that had fallen to the ground and ripped it open before she handed it to him. She didn't think he'd gotten caught up. She was starting to think he didn't have any money. She almost felt sorry for him. "Here. Don't worry about paying for it. Just eat."

He took the candy, and then a bite. "You're too kind." He looked up for a second.

Blue eyes. A vibrant blue. Blond hair, wispy and nearly white really. Not with age, just a very, very light shade of blond. His nose was crooked. To the left.

"Didn't expect to run across someone so young and pretty in a tiny little Wyoming town."

"Uh—"

"Sorry." He looked back down at the candy bar, the brim of his hat hiding everything again. "That's awkward and uncomfortable. Let's blame it on the lack of food. Do you think I could trouble you for a small sip of water?"

Jen jumped to her feet and hurried for the cooler that boasted rows of water bottles. She grabbed one of the larger ones and twisted it open. "Here," she said, returning to his side. "You just take this."

He took a sip and then nodded, using the back of his arm to wipe the water droplets off his mouth. He kept his head down.

Was it purposeful? Was he trying to make sure she couldn't identify him? Was he planning something awful? But she'd seen his eyes and the color of his hair—she only had to remember the details.

He took another bite of the candy bar, then a drink of the water. She racked her brain trying to figure out what to do. How to defend herself if he lunged at her. This could all be an act. A ploy. Weaken her defenses, catch her off guard.

Carefully, Jen leaned slightly away and got to her feet, keeping her eyes on him and her body tense and ready to react.

"Thank you for the kindness," he said, sounding exhausted. But it *could* be acting. "I should be out of your way." He struggled to his feet, swayed again, but righted himself.

He seemed so genuinely thankful and feeble. The man was a mess, and maybe he *was* Ty's threatening stranger, but he wasn't doing anything to put her in danger at the moment.

And why would he? He was probably just after Ty. How could she blame anyone on that front?

"Can I get you anything else? Maybe a sandwich? A bag of chips?" His clear weakness ate at her. A man shouldn't go hungry. Though, she supposed, he could sell that nice camera if he was really that bad off.

"No. No, I'll be fine." He kept his head tilted away, but the corner of his smile was soft and kind as he lifted the water bottle in salute. "I appreciate it, ma'am. Your kindness won't be forgotten." And with that, he walked out of the store. No trouble. No danger.

Leaving Jen unsure about what to do.

TY DIDN'T OFTEN find himself uncomfortable. He'd learned early to roll with whatever punches life threw at him. There'd been quite a few.

But nothing could have prepared him for a baby shower. A Carson-Delaney baby shower. Laurel and Vanessa were laughing over their baby bumps, pastel pink and blue decorations everywhere, and Carsons and Delaneys mingled like there'd never been a feud.

Jen was in a corner talking to Addie and Noah, Addie's toddler trying to crawl up Noah and laughing hysterically when he fell. Noah watched with the patience of a happy man.

Ty had never particularly understood his brother, though he loved him with a fierceness that meant he'd lay down his life for the man. What he did know about Noah was that having Addie and Seth in his life and on his ranch made him happy, and that was all Ty really cared about.

"Delaney Delirium getting to you?"

Ty gave Grady a cool look. "Just trying to understand all this baby business," he said, nodding toward Noah and the way he held Seth easily on his hip.

Grady patted him on the back. Hard. "Sure, buddy."

"You really want to be a dad after the way we grew up?" Ty asked, unable to stop himself. He didn't get it. The way Noah had taken to Addic's nephew that she was guardian and mother to, as if it were easy to step into the role of guardian and father. The way Vanessa and Grady seemed calm and even happy about their impending parenthood.

The Carson generation before theirs had not

been a particular parental one. More fists and threats than nurturing happiness.

"Figure I got a pretty good example of what *not* to do," Grady said with a shrug. "And a woman to knock some sense into me when I make mistakes. Besides, we turned out okay in spite of it all."

"And Delaney senior ain't got a problem with his grandchild being raised by a cop and saloon owner?"

"Laurel's father doesn't get a say."

Ty knew it was different for Grady. Ty had been eighteen when Mr. Delaney had flexed his parental and town muscles to make sure Ty got the hell away from his daughter. Grady wasn't a dumb teenager, and neither was Laurel. They could refuse a parent's interference.

Couldn't you have?

He shook his head. Ancient history. No amount of Carson and Delaney comingling was reason to go back there.

Laurel called Grady over and he left Ty in the middle of all this goodwill and pastel baby nonsense. He was somewhere in no-man's land. He almost wished a sniper would take him out.

There were toasts and cake and presents of tiny clothes and board books. No matter that their families had been enemies for over a century, no matter that people in town still whispered about curses and the inevitable terrible ends they would all meet, Carsons and Delaneys sat together celebrating new lives.

Some unknown ache spread through him. He couldn't name it, and he couldn't seem to force it away. It sat in his gut, throbbing out to all his limbs.

Faking his best smile, he went to Vanessa and Grady and made his half-hearted excuses to leave early. No one stopped him, but his family sure watched him slip out the front door. He could feel their eyes, their questions. And worst of all, their pity.

As if being alone was the worst fate a person could face. He'd seen a lot worse. This was fine. And good. Right for him. Alone suited—

"Ty."

There was something his gut did when she said his name. No matter the years, he couldn't seem to control that intrinsic physical reaction to his name forming on her lips. A softening. A longing.

He took a minute to brace himself before he turned around. Jen stood on the porch of Grady and Laurel's cabin. She looked like cotton candy in some lacy, frothy pink thing.

And all too viscerally he could remember what she looked like completely *unclothed.* No matter that he assured himself time changed things—bodies, minds, hearts. It was hard to remember as she approached him with a face that wasn't shooting daggers at him for the first time since he'd arrived home.

"Listen." She looked back at the open door, then took a few more steps toward him on the walk. "I wanted to let you know I had a stranger come in the store last night."

"What?" he demanded, fury easily taking over the ache inside him. *Last night?* "Why didn't you call me? I told you—"

She lifted her chin, her eyes cold as ice. "You told me to let you know. Here I am, letting you know. I don't think he's whatever you're looking for. He was perfectly nice. He just asked to take pictures of the store, and then he—"

"What time did he come in?"

"Well, seven but—"

"He was going to take pictures when it was pitch-black?"

She frowned at that, a line forming between her brows that once upon a time he'd loved tracing with his thumb. Where had *that* memory come from?

"He was hungry. He *fainted.* He was out of it. Confused maybe. And totally polite and harmless."

"Damn it, Jen. I told you to call me. I could have—"

"He didn't *do* anything. I know you're paranoid, but—"

"I am *not* paranoid. You think a man who gets a letter with no postage delivered to where he lives and works is paranoid?"

She tilted her head, studying him, and he realized with a start he'd said too much.

He never said too much.

"What was in the letter?" she asked, her voice calm and her eyes on him.

It was hell, this. Still wanting her. Missing that old tiny slice of his life where she'd been his. He didn't want this, but he couldn't seem to get rid of it. It ate at him, had him dreaming about doing things he couldn't possibly allow himself to do. Every once in a while he'd think...what would just one touch do?

But he knew the answer to that.

She audibly swallowed and looked away, a faint blush staining her cheeks. She felt it, too, and yet...

"It doesn't matter," he grumbled, trying to find his usual center of calm. His normal, everyday clear-eyed view of the world and of this problem he had. "What did he look like? Better yet—I want to see your security tape."

Her eyes flashed anger and frustration. "You are *not* looking at my security tape."

"Why not?"

"It's an invasion of my customers' privacy."

He snorted. "I don't care that Mary Lynn Jones bought a pack of Marlboros even though her husband thinks she quit or that little Adam Teller was buying condoms because he talked his way into Lizzie Granger's pants."

Jen's mouth twitched, but then she firmed it into a scowl. "How do you know all that?"

"I pay attention, babe."

Her scowl deepened and she folded her arms across her chest. "Blond hair, blue eyes. About the same height as Cam. I'm not sure what that'd be in feet and inches, but I imagine you would. Skinny, but strong, like a marathon runner. He wore hiking clothes and boots, all in tan, and a big, fancy camera around his neck. Topped it off with a Stetson. Said he was taking pictures of ghost towns and happened upon Bent."

It was more to go on than he thought he'd get out of her, but still not enough to ring any bells. "Tattoos? Scars? Something off about him?"

She shook her head. "Not that I could see."

"I want the tape, Jen. If someone is..." He didn't want to tell her. Didn't trust her to keep it a secret and let him handle it, but he needed to see the man himself. Needed to identify him so he could neutralize this threat. "I'm getting letters. They're not threatening exactly, but they're not...not. I know you don't care about me, but your family is all tangled up with mine now." He gestured at the whole irritating lot of them. "Don't you want to protect what's yours?"

"Of course I do."

That sharp chin of hers came up, defiant and angry. Her temper used to amuse him. Now it just made that ache center in his heart.

But that wasn't the problem at hand. "Then let me see the tape. If I recognize him, I'll know what to do. If I don't, then maybe you're right and it's harmless coincidence." He didn't believe that, but he'd let her think he did.

She was quiet and stiff for humming seconds, then finally she sighed. "Oh, fine. I suppose you want to go now?"

He only raised an eyebrow.

She rolled her eyes. "Let me get my purse and say my goodbyes." She stalked back inside, grumbling about irritating, stubborn males the whole way up.

All Ty could do was pray he'd recognize whoever was on that tape and everything would be over.

Jen stepped out of her tiny little sedan, dressed all in pink, her dark hair in pretty waves around her shoulders.

Sweet. Just like Ty had said. She'd been wary of him last night when he'd first walked into the store. He'd seen it in her eyes, but the feigned hunger and stumble had softened her. She'd given him food and water. Good-hearted, she was indeed.

He smiled, watching as Jen stood there in front of her store. When a motorcycle roared into view, his smile died.

Even before the man took off his helmet, he knew who it was. He watched Jen. She didn't seem *happy* to see Ty, but nor did she seem surprised or *un*happy.

He scowled, watching as Ty strode over to Jen. They exchanged a few words and then Jen unlocked the store and stepped inside, Ty right behind her.

She didn't flip the sign from Closed to Open.

He narrowed his eyes. The rage that slammed into him was sudden and violent, but he'd learned a thing or two about how to handle it. Hone it.

Ty would get his. He *would.*

So, patience would be the name of the game. And another letter.

This time in blood.

Chapter Three

Jen set her purse down on her desk in the back room of the store and tried not to sigh. Why was she getting involved in this?

Don't you want to protect what's yours?

It grated all over again. That he could even ask her that. She would have protected *him*, sacrificed for *him*, and he'd left her alone and confused and so brokenhearted she'd…

She booted up her computer, stabbing at the buttons in irritation. She'd eradicate the past if she could, but since she couldn't she had to find a better way of managing her reaction to it in Ty's presence.

Looming over her like some hulking specter. She flicked a glance over her shoulder and up. "Do you mind?"

His eyes were hard and his mouth was harder. He was taking this so seriously, and that irritated her. Ty was never serious. Oh, deep down he was, but he usually masked it with lazy smiles and sarcastic remarks.

But whatever this was had him giving no pretense of humor.

She focused on the computer and brought up the security footage. She ignored the flutter of panic in her throat, dismissed it as foolish. Whatever was going on was Ty's problem, and once she showed him the footage he'd realize that and leave her alone.

She fast-forwarded through the day, moving the cursor to around seven when the man had come in. She zipped through her conversation with Jim and his case of beer, then hit Play when the door opened after Jim's exit.

They both watched in silence, heads nearly together as they studied the video.

"You can't see him," Ty said flatly, his breath making the hair at her ear dance. She ignored the shiver of reaction and made sure her voice was even before she spoke.

"Give it a second."

They continued to watch, and Jen could only hope Ty was so focused on the video he didn't notice the goose bumps on her arm or the way her breathing wasn't exactly even.

She had to fight viciously against the memories that wanted to worm their way into her consciousness. Memories of them together. Close like this. Not at *all* clothed like this.

But it was silence around them, heavy, pregnant silence, and she didn't dare look to see if Ty was keeping his eyes on the computer. Of course he was. That's what they were here for.

"You can't see his face," Ty repeated.

Jen peered at the form on the screen. She saw herself, watching the man's entrance. And everywhere the man moved, his hat obscured his face from the camera.

"He did it on purpose."

"How would he have known where the camera is?" Jen returned. It was so natural, the way the stranger on the video kept his head down. She wanted to believe Ty was overreacting, but an uncomfortable feeling itched along her spine.

"He did it on purpose," Ty said in that same flat tone.

"Keep watching. We'll get a glimpse when he falls."

But as the man on the screen pitched forward into the candy, and then staggered back before falling to the ground, his face remained completely hidden by the hat.

Jen frowned at that. But surely a man who fell over didn't *purposefully* shield himself from a security camera. It was just coincidence.

"Rewind it," Ty ordered.

She opened her mouth to tell him not to order her around, but then huffed out a breath. Why bother arguing with a brick wall? She moved the cursor back to the man's entrance, then slowed down the time.

Nothing changed. You couldn't see the guy's face. But she let Ty watch. She turned to study him. He was so close her nose all but brushed his cheek. If he noticed, he didn't show it. His gaze was flat and blank, seeing nothing but the computer screen.

His profile could be so hard. *He* could be so hard, but there'd been softness and kindness underneath that mask all those years ago. Did it still exist? Or had military life sucked it out of him? Were any of the parts of him that she loved still in there, or were they all gone?

Horrified with that thought, she blinked at the stinging in her eyes. Stupid. It didn't matter one way or the other. Yes, he'd broken her heart years ago, but she'd gotten over it. She'd moved on. And he definitely had.

So, her brain needed to stop taking detours to the past.

"He faked that fall," Ty said, as if it was fact, not just his insane opinion on the matter.

"You're being paranoid."

He turned his head so fast she startled back. His eyes were blazing blue, and no matter how tightly he held his jaw, his mouth was soft. She knew exactly what it would feel like on hers.

What the hell was wrong with her? She closed her eyes against the heated wave of embarrassment.

"I am not being paranoid," he said, his voice low and controlled. "I'm being rational. I'm putting all the dots together. That man didn't fall because he was starving. Did you see that fancy camera? He can afford to eat."

She opened her eyes, irritation exceeding embarrassment and old stupid feelings. "That doesn't mean—"

"And furthermore," Ty said, getting in her face no matter how she leaned away in her chair, "even if he *did* fall, he kept his face away from that camera for a reason. I *know* it. Now, you want to prove it, you watch hours of your own security tape and see if that happens with any other person."

He held her gaze, though after a while some of that furious, righteous anger softened into something else. Something… *Something* as his blue eyes roamed her face, settled on her mouth.

Jen shot out of the chair, ignoring the fact she bumped into him, and then scrambled away. "I…have to open the store," she stuttered. "Everyone's expecting me to open at three." She was being foolish, but her heart was hammering in her throat and she had to get out of this tiny room where Ty loomed far too large.

He stood, blocking the door, still as a rock, eyeing her carefully. "You have to be careful, Jen."

She fisted her hands on her hips. "He isn't after me. Now let me out."

"He came in here. He talked to you. There's something purposeful in that."

"What do *I* have to do with your threatening letters?"

He heaved out a breath. "Look." He shook his head, crossed his arms over his chest. He looked at the ceiling, then dropped his arms and shoved his hands in his pockets.

She raised her eyebrows. Nerves? No, not exactly, but definitely discomfort. She wasn't sure she'd ever seen Ty something like unsure.

"I have a feeling this ties to someone I was in the military with," he said, sounding disgusted with himself.

"Again, what does that have to do with me?"

"If it's someone I knew? Someone I bunked with? They would have listened to me talk about home, about my family, about…" He nodded in her direction.

She could only blink at him. He'd talked about *her*? After leaving her like she was garbage you dumped on the side of the road? It didn't make any sense.

"I can't tell anything from that tape, but I've got threatening letters and a strange man in your store, so I've got to think of the obvious conclusion here. You could be in danger."

"That's absurd," she responded. It had to be.

He stepped forward, and before she could sidestep him, he took her by the chin. Her whole body zoomed off into some other dimension she hadn't been to in a very long time. She could only stare at him, while his big, rough hand held her face in place.

"I need you to be careful." He was so solemn, so serious.

Her throat constricted and her heart beat so hard she was sure her whole body vibrated from the violence of it.

His grip on her chin softened, his fingertip moving along the line of her jaw. She wanted to melt into a puddle, but she wasn't seventeen anymore, and with that fission of delight she was reminded she *hated* Ty Carson.

She slapped his hand away, raising her chin at him, trying for regal instead of panicked. "Don't manhandle me."

He only raised an eyebrow.

"I don't know what you want from me," she

said, with more feeling than she should have shown him.

"I want you to be aware. Take precautions. Keep yourself safe and protected, and if that man comes in your store again, I want you to call me immediately." He moved out of the way of the door and her exit. "It's that simple."

Simple? Sure. As if anything to do with Ty Carson was *simple*.

TY WALKED OUT of the general store knowing he'd overplayed his hand. Disgusted with himself for getting wrapped up in old feelings and memories and not focusing on the task at hand, he stalked to his motorcycle.

But he couldn't eradicate the look of Jen's brown eyes, wide on his, her mouth open in shock as he'd held her face. The flutter of pulse. It felt as though in that moment a million memories had arced between them.

He tried to shake it off. They weren't the same people. He had regrets, sure. He should have handled everything with her father differently. But he hadn't and there was no reason to beat himself up over it. You couldn't change the past.

And he couldn't change the fact being a soldier and away from home for nearly a decade with only sporadic visits when on leave had altered him. He wasn't the same teenager who'd run off when the right pressure was applied. Even though Jen had stayed in Bent, she wasn't the same girl.

They were different people, and if there was still a physical attraction it would be best if they both ignored it.

But even more important than that, he had to protect her from whatever was going on. He wasn't sure how to do that yet, but he knew he had to figure it out.

He almost ran right into someone, so lost in his own irritable thoughts. He opened his mouth to apologize, until he recognized the middle-aged man before him.

Mr. Delaney's eyes went from the store, to Ty, and then went hard and flat. "I hope you know what you're doing, Carson."

Funny how time didn't change the utter authority in this man's voice. Jen's father thought he owned the *world*, and Ty was sick with regret for ever being a part of that certainty.

"Know what I'm doing? Hmm." Ty smiled. "I suppose I always do."

"You'll watch your step where my daughter is concerned."

Ty raised an eyebrow and looked back at the store himself. Then he let his smile widen into a wolfish grin.

"I got rid of you once, Tyler. I don't know why I couldn't do it again."

Ty didn't let the violent fury show. He wouldn't give this man the satisfaction. He kept the smile in place, made sure his voice was lazy, but with enough edge to carry a threat. "I seem to recall you fooling around with a married woman, Delaney. I wonder what other dirty skeletons are rattling around in your closet. More torrid connections to other Carsons? Or are your kids taking care of that these days?"

It irritated Ty that not even a flicker of that blow hitting showed on Delaney's face, though he knew it was at least a little knock to the man's pride. That it had come out he'd had an affair with a woman who'd been married to someone else. And not just that, a woman who was blood related to Ty himself.

"Your cousins have made my children very happy," Delaney said, surprising the hell out of Ty. "Maybe you shouldn't have run away all those years ago." He smiled pleasantly. "But you did. The kind of running away that isn't so easy to forgive."

Ty kept his smile in place by sheer force of will. He'd faced down his father's fists. He had no trouble facing down Delaney's barbs. "Funny thing about coming back home again." He glanced at the store. "Some things never change, and some people are more forgiving than others."

Finally he got a reaction out of Delaney, though it was only a tightening of his jaw. Still, it was better than nothing. "Impending grand-parenthood looks good on you, Delaney. Have a nice day." He patted the man's shoulder, gratified when Delaney jerked away and stalked into the store.

To Jen. Ty sighed. The simple truth was he had more to worry about than Jen or her father. He had to worry about the messages he was receiving, the uncomfortable gut feeling he had that Jen was in danger. Because of him.

The most important thing was keeping her safe. Not because he still had feelings for her, but because it was the right thing to do. The timing of the letter, the mention of first loves and this stranger's appearance in the store were too close to be coincidental or for him to believe Jen wasn't a target.

If this connected to his military days—which were the only days he'd spent away from Bent—and Jen was a target, it would have to be from early in his career. Before the rangers.

He racked his brain for someone he'd wronged, someone he'd had friction with. A few superiors, but nothing personal. Just normal army stuff, and he'd hardly been the only soldier who'd occasionally mouthed off and gotten punished for it. There'd been the man he'd ratted out, but the man on the tape wasn't Oscar. Not even close. Besides, Oscar had to have known his time in the army was limited when he couldn't keep himself out of the booze or drugs.

Ty brought to mind the figure from Jen's security tape. Not even a tingle of recognition. It ate at him, the faceless man manipulating Jen in her own store. It damn near burned him alive to think she'd be a target of something she had nothing to do with.

Target or not, her cooperation or not, he'd keep her safe. He just had to figure out how.

HE DIDN'T MIND cutting himself. He rather liked it. Watching the blood well up, drip down. He'd always liked blood. Dr. Michaels said he had to be careful, not to get too caught up in it.

She was right. He only had so much time. Ty would stay at the store for only so long, and it would take time to sneak into Rightful Claim. He had to craft his message quickly, then deliver it with just as much precision and speed.

The paper hadn't worked, so he'd torn off a piece of his T-shirt and concentrated carefully as he used his bloody fingertip to spell out the message.

He admired his work. He supposed blood

might tell, giving away his identity, but he wasn't so worried about that. He liked the message of blood too much to worry about the connections.

Besides, by the time blood told, he'd have his revenge.

Chapter Four

Jen had done a lot of pretending in her life. All through high school she'd pretended she wasn't involved with Ty Carson, then after he'd left she'd pretended she wasn't heartbroken. She did her best to pretend Laurel's marriage to Grady and Dylan's marriage to Vanessa didn't bother her. For most of her life, she'd fooled those she loved the most.

She didn't think she'd fooled anyone tonight as she'd pretended to cheerfully spend her evening making dinner for her family at the Delaney Ranch. She'd chattered happily through dinner, then cleaned up diligently, refusing help and earning looks.

Pity looks.

Even though Ty's whole *thing* was giving her the constant creeps and a feeling of being watched, she went home to her apartment above the store after tidying up at Delaney Ranch. She'd rather face off with someone who might be "targeting" her than withstand her family's pity—most especially the in-law Carson portion of her "family."

Jen always passed the storefront on Main before pulling into the alley where stairs led up to her apartment behind the store. No matter what time of day, she always scanned the front to make sure everything was as it should be.

Her heart slammed painfully against her chest at the shadowy figure looming under the awning of the store's front door, highlighted by the faint security lights inside. She whipped her gaze from the door to the road, jerking the wheel to miss the sidewalk she'd been about to careen onto.

Heart pounding, palms sweating, Jen kept driving, taking her normal turn onto the alley. What should she do? Who was lurking outside her store?

It could be anyone. Jim wanted a six-pack. Someone taking an evening stroll. It could be nothing. But it felt like something.

She fished her phone out of her purse, debating whether she should park or keep driving. The person had to have seen her erratic driving. Would whomever it was know who she was? Would the individual walk back here? Threaten her?

"Oh, damn you, Ty Carson." She pushed the

car into Park, watching the alley in case anyone appeared. She started to dial Ty, then cursed herself for it. A smart woman didn't call the idiotic, paranoid man who was causing her panic in the first place. A smart woman called the cops.

And lucky for her, her sister was the cops.

Except Laurel was a detective. And pregnant. *Don't you want to protect what's yours?* She cursed Ty all over again, staring at her phone with indecision. Laurel or Ty? Bent County Sheriff's Department or handle this herself?

She looked back up at the alley entrance. There was no sign of anyone. Surely someone nefarious would have run away upon being spotted. She wouldn't be foolish when everyone already pitied her. No.

Quickly and decisively, she got out of her car and hurried to the back door of the store. She watched the alley, fumbling with her keys as she worked to get the door open. Once inside she quickly shut it and locked it behind her, taking a deep breath and trying to steady her shaky limbs.

"You're being ridiculous," she muttered into the empty room. Still, her heartbeat didn't calm and her nerves continued to fray as she moved from the back of the store to the front. At first she didn't see anything, then a shadow moved and she barely held back the impulse to scream.

It was the man who'd fainted in her store.

Despite all the assurances she'd given Ty that the stranger was no one and completely non-threatening, *this* felt very threatening.

She backed away from the door, pulling her phone out of her purse. Quickly, she dialed the dispatch number for the sheriff's department. When a woman answered, she explained as calmly and concisely as she could that someone was outside her store, and she didn't consider him dangerous but she did have some concerns.

"I'll have a deputy out your way as soon as possible, ma'am."

"Thank you." Jen hit End and then steeled herself to turn around. He was still there, which had her breath coming in quick puffs. He wasn't pounding on the door or the storefront glass. He was simply standing there, same as he had been.

Except, she realized, he was holding something against the window of the door. Unsteady, Jen inched toward the door, realizing it was a piece of paper. He was holding something like a sign against the glass.

In careful print, it read: *I only wanted to thank you for the other day.*

Though the soft security lights from inside the store lit up the boardwalk enough to illuminate him, he had his cowboy hat pulled low. He smiled sheepishly and it sent a tickle of panic through her that his mouth was the only part of him she could make out.

"I called the police," she shouted, wondering if the sound would carry through the glass.

His sheepish smile didn't fade, but he did nod. He pulled a pen out of his pocket and began to write on the paper again. When he flipped it around, she had to squint and step a little closer to read it.

Didn't mean to frighten you. I'll be on my way. See you soon, Jen.

Jen.

He'd written her name, clear as day. Why did he know her name?

He could have overheard it. He could have asked around. Neither made her feel comforted.

She noticed the flash of red and blue lights. She craned her head to see the cruiser's progress with some relief easing away the panic.

But when she looked back at the door the man was gone, and dread pooled inside her stomach.

None of it was threatening, and yet she felt threatened. Chilled to the bone. She hugged herself as she waited for the deputy to get out of his cruiser and walk up to the door.

She forced herself to smile at him when she opened the door to him. Thanks to her sister's position with the sheriff's department, she knew most of the deputies. Thomas better than most. "Thomas, thanks for coming, but I feel a little silly. He went away without any fuss."

"It's no problem, Jen. Better safe than sorry, and you know your sister would have my butt if I didn't check it out. Now, why don't you tell me everything that happened."

She sighed, knowing it would all get back to Laurel, and she'd have to answer a thousand questions. Knowing Laurel would tell Grady, who'd undoubtedly mention it to Ty. She'd have to tell Ty herself in that case.

She faced that with about as much dread as she had the stranger at her door.

TY YAWNED, FEELING unaccountably tired for an early Sunday night. Rightful Claim closed down at midnight rather than two, and he should have felt revved.

Instead, the lack of sleep over the past few days was getting to him. Was he getting old? He shook his head, pushing his apartment door open.

Something fluttered at his feet and he knew immediately it would be another note. He bent down to pick it up, but the odd shape and color of the letters stopped him midcrouch. Icy cold settled in his gut and spread through his limbs.

It was blood. Even as he warned himself it could be fake, he knew. It was blood. A message written in blood.

It wasn't hard to access the part of his brain he'd spent a decade honing in the army and the army rangers. It clicked into place like a machine switched on.

He stood to his full height, taking a careful step backward. The less he disturbed the scene, the better chance he had of nipping this all in the bud before anyone got hurt.

Jen. He pulled the phone out of his pocket and dialed her number. He refused to put her as a contact in his phone, but he knew the number nevertheless. All it had taken was Laurel insisting her wedding party had each other's phone numbers to have it lodged in his brain like a tumor.

It rang, ending on her voice mail message. She was probably asleep, but it didn't assuage his fear. He left a terse message. "Call me. ASAP."

He clicked End and pushed away that jangle of worry. Once he took care of this, he'd make sure she was fast asleep. He'd make sure, wherever she was and whatever she was doing, she was safe and sound.

Safe.

Ty looked at his phone and couldn't believe

what he was about to do. He was a Carson and Carsons handled their own stuff, but with Jen involved for whatever reason, he couldn't take that chance.

Because Jen *was* involved, he knew that. Even without reading this new message. He knew the man trying to frighten him would use Jen to do it.

So, he called the Bent County Sheriff's Department. He explained the situation and was assured someone would be over shortly.

Then he called Jen again, cursing her refusal to answer. *She's asleep and has her phone on silent.*

"Screw it," he muttered, moving out of his apartment and back down the stairs. If he walked around to the front of the saloon, he'd be able to see her store. He knew he should wait for the cops, but if her security lights were on, if he jogged over and checked to make sure her car was in the back lot…

Of course, she might have spent the night at the Delaney Ranch. Jen didn't keep a regular schedule, which was going to be a problem if he was going to keep her safe. Not that he could force her to change anything. She'd only get more erratic if he warned her to stay in one place.

Hardheaded woman.

He stepped outside and his heart all but stopped. The flashing lights of a police cruiser were across the road and down the street, right in front of Delaney General.

Without thinking it through, he was ready to run down the street, bust in and save her from whatever was wrong.

But his name broke through the haze.

"Carson?"

Ty whirled to face the cop walking toward him. Younger guy. Ty didn't like cops, period, but if he had to deal with one he would have preferred Hart. Ty was pretty sure this was the one who'd nearly bungled Addie's kidnapping last year.

"What?" Ty barked. "What's going on over there?"

"Nothing serious. Just a suspicious figure. But you put in a call, too. Something about a note?"

Ty looked at the car down by Delaney General, and then at the too-young deputy trying to be tough.

Ty felt his age for a moment, not in years, but in the decade he'd spent in the military. He remembered what it was like to be young and eager. Foolishly sure of his role in helping people. No doubt this moron had the same conviction, and someday it would be beaten out of him.

Ty tried to keep his voice from being a harsh demand. “So, everyone’s okay down there?”

“Looks like it was innocent and harmless. Spooked Ms. Delaney some, but no real threat. We’ve canvassed the area for a while now, with no evidence of anyone. We were just finishing up when we got your call on the radio. Now, why don’t you show me the note.”

“Who’s with her?”

“Hart.”

Ty nodded. That was good. That was fine. Let the police take care of Jen. *Suspicious figure.* Ty looked around Main Street, mostly pitch-black except for the occasional glow from nearby businesses’ security lights.

Someone was out there. A suspicious figure.

“Carson?”

“Right. Upstairs. You got stuff to collect it or whatever? I’m pretty sure it’s written in blood.”

The deputy’s eyebrows rose, but he nodded. “I’ve got everything I need to handle it.” He patted his utility belt and then followed Ty around the bar and into the back entrance.

Ty led him to the letter, and the deputy crouched and pulled on rubber gloves as he examined it. “Is this the first letter you’ve received like this?”

"It's the first one in blood, but it isn't the first one."

The deputy spared him a look. One that said *and you're just now calling the police?* It was only his worry over Jen and her suspicious figure that kept him from kicking the cop out and telling him he'd handle it faster and better.

The deputy picked it up and slid it into what looked like a ziplock bag.

"What's it say?" Ty demanded.

The deputy stood and raised his eyebrows. "You didn't read it?"

"I didn't want to touch it. Blood or fingerprints… You'll be able to get something off it?"

"Should be. Blood could be animal, but there might be something here. Though it'll take some time to send that off for analysis."

"But you will?"

"I'll be recommending it," the deputy returned with a nod. "This is a serious threat." He held up the bag and read through it. "I'd warn you to watch your back, but it won't be your back I'm after."

Jen. He didn't know why this person was fixating on Jen, but he was sure of it. "We need to know who that is."

"You don't have any clues?"

"None. Someone from my army days, maybe?

But I'm in the dark. If we can get DNA off that—"

"What about the other letters? Where are they?"

Struggling between his need to do this on his own and his understanding he needed the cops in on this if Jen was going to stay safe, Ty stalked over to the kitchen drawer he'd shoved the other letters in. He grabbed them and held them out to the deputy.

The deputy took them, then nodded toward the door as footfalls sounded on the stairs. "That'll be Hart. We'll want to consider the connection angle on this. A note to you, a threatening figure at Ms. Delaney's store. Same time frame."

It was indeed Hart, but Ty frowned at Jen walking into the room behind him.

"What's going on?" Jen demanded. "Was he here, too?"

Hart turned to Jen, placed a gentle hand on her shoulder. Gentle enough that Ty's eyes narrowed.

"Jen," Hart said quietly. "Maybe you should calm—"

"Don't you dare tell me to calm down, Thomas." Jen shrugged off his hand and glared at him, then Ty. "Ty seems to think this man is connected—the one sending him threatening notes, and the stranger at my store. And you told me he got another one. Well, it's not okay, and I'm somehow involved. I want to know why."

"We don't know it's the same person," the deputy with the letters said to Hart and Jen. "We only know it's suspicious timing. Do you have an idea of when the letter was dropped off?"

Ty sighed. "I've been bartending since four. Didn't come up till after midnight. I don't know how someone would have broken in without me noticing anything, but it could have happened anytime."

Hart jotted something down on a notepad while the other deputy read through the notes Ty had handed him.

"Excuse us a moment," Hart said, nodding to the other deputy into the hallway. They stood there, conferring in low tones.

Ty studied Jen. She looked calm and collected, pretty as a picture considering it was the middle of the night and she'd called the police over a suspicious figure.

"You and Hart got a thing?" Ty asked, harsher than he'd intended, and if he'd been thinking at all he wouldn't have asked. But the way Hart had touched her raked along his skin like nails on a chalkboard. He didn't like it.

She blinked, looked up at him as though he'd lost his mind. "A thing?"

Ty probably *had* lost his mind, but he wasn't going to let her see that. So he shrugged lazily. "You're the only one I've ever heard call him Thomas. I was starting to think his first name *was* Hart."

"Oh. Well."

"So, you have a thing." He didn't ask it. He stated it. Because of course they did. Delaneys loved their law and order.

Any embarrassment or discomfort she'd had on her face morphed into full-on bristle. "It's none of your business, is it?"

Ty shrugged, forcing the move to be negligent even though his shoulders felt like iron. "It is if he's got a vested interest in keeping you safe. Make it easier for me to trust him anyhow."

"You don't need to worry about me, Tyler."

He tried not to scowl, since she was clearly trying to irritate him, but his name was one of the few things that irritated him no matter how hard he tried to let it go. "If something I did brought you danger, I'll worry about you as much as I want."

She softened at that some. "Ty—"

He didn't want her softening. "You need to stay with your family until this is sorted. The cops might look into it, but they're useless. With the exception of maybe your boyfriend there. This is escalating, and you need to be protected."

"Because heaven forbid I protect myself?"

"Honey, you're Bambi in the woods full of wolves. Stay at that mansion of yours where your brothers can keep an eye on you."

"My *brothers*. Right. Because only men can protect."

"They've got some military experience. That isn't sexism. It's reality."

"The reality is Laurel's a police officer, and I know how to handle myself."

"Laurel's pregnant," Ty responded simply. "You really want her keeping your butt out of trouble?"

"My *butt* is in trouble because of *you*, somehow. You leave without a peep, disappear into thin air, leaving me…" She sucked in a breath and closed her eyes. "You know what? Ancient history doesn't matter. You got me into this mess, and I expect *you* to get me out. Not my brothers, not the police—you."

He looked down at her grimly, then forced himself to smile. "You sure you want that, babe?"

She scowled at him, shaking her hair back

like a woman ready to kick some butt. "And why wouldn't I?"

Hart stepped back in, eyeing them both with something like consideration. "We'll take this back to the station, see what kind of analysis we can get. I'd caution you both to be careful, and call me or Deputy McCarthy if you think of anything that might help us figure out the identity of either the suspicious figure or the person writing the notes."

Ty nodded and Jen sent Hart a sweet smile. "Of course."

"Do you want me to escort you back to your store, Jen?" Hart asked.

Jen sent Ty a killing look, then beamed at Hart. "Thank you, Thomas. I'd appreciate that." She strode over to him, and they walked out of Ty's apartment chatting in low tones.

Deputy McCarthy tipped his hat at Ty. "Call if you think of anything, and we'll be in touch."

Ty only grunted, paying more attention to Hart's and Jen's retreating backs than McCarthy's words.

If she had Hart wrapped around her finger, she'd be fine. Safe. Watched after by more than just her cop sister who was busy growing a human being inside her. He should stop worrying. Jen was a Delaney and would be protected at all costs, regardless of what Ty did.

But no matter how hard he tried to convince himself of that, the worry didn't go away.

HE LIKED WATCHING the police lights flash red and blue. He liked knowing he'd caused a few scenes, and there was a hot lick of thrill at the idea everyone was thinking about him, trying to figure out who he was and what he wanted.

He slunk through the shadows, evading the stupid, useless cops with ease. Watching, always watching.

He'd had a moment of rage when Jen had hurried toward Ty's place with the cop. She'd looked worried.

The cop had touched her.

Now they were walking back out of Ty's. They smiled at each other. The other cop exited shortly thereafter, but the first cop stayed by Jen's side as they walked back to her store.

He followed, melting into the shadows, watching. Jen touched the cop's arm, and he could all but read her lips.

Thank you.

No. This wouldn't do. Jen was his now. His quarry and his to do with whatever he wanted. Part revenge, yes. Hurt Ty. His first objective was always to hurt Ty.

But Jen was pretty and sweet. She had a nice smile. He didn't want her just to hurt Ty anymore, he wanted her. She would be his prize when he tipped the scales back. When he had revenge, he'd have Jen, too.

This cop wouldn't do. Not at all.

Chapter Five

Jen was exhausted when her alarm went off the next morning. Exhausted and then irritated when she knew, without even getting up, that someone was in her apartment.

She might have been scared if she didn't know her family so well, or if she didn't smell what she assumed was Laurel's "famous" omelet—i.e., the only thing she ever bothered to cook.

Jen grabbed her fluffy pink robe that so often brought her comfort and slipped it on as she got out of bed. Summer was beginning to fade, and mornings were colder every day.

Jen moved from her bedroom to the small cramped space of living room and kitchen. "This better be a bad dream," she said, glaring at her sister.

Laurel raised an eyebrow at her as she flipped the omelet in the skillet. "You're telling me."

"Thomas shouldn't have called you." She'd

known he would, but he *shouldn't* have. It was at least a small part of the reason the few dates she'd been on with him hadn't worked out. He all but idolized her sister as a police officer, and whether it was petty or not, Jen had never been completely comfortable with it.

"Hart knew better than to keep it from me. I'd have heard about it when I got into the station later, if not before." Laurel turned her attention back to the eggs, and her tone was purposefully mild. "I thought it didn't work out between you two."

Laurel was only ten months older than her, and they'd grown up not just as sisters, but also as friends. Still, ever since high school there'd been this Ty-sized distance between them. Because Jen hadn't told *anyone* about Ty, even her sister. Jen had always known Laurel felt it, and yet she'd never been able to cross that distance. She'd been too embarrassed.

Jen moved into the kitchen, hating the way all this ancient history swirled around her no matter what she did. "It didn't work out with Thomas."

"Then why do you still call him Thomas?"

"Because I wanted it to." Jen sank into her kitchen chair, giving up on sending her sister home. She raked her hands through her hair. "Can't you tell your husband to send his cousin back to wherever he came from and stop ruining my life?"

"So, it didn't work out with Hart because of Ty?"

"No, that isn't what I'm saying." Frowning at Laurel's back, Jen worked through that. "What would Ty have to do with me dating Thomas?"

Laurel shrugged. "I always suspected… Well, something." Laurel moved the omelet onto a plate before turning to face Jen and sliding it in front of her. "Why don't you tell me the truth?"

Jen should. Ty was old news, and it didn't matter now. He'd left. She'd gotten over it. Why not tell her sister? What she'd done in her teens shouldn't be embarrassing in her late twenties. "It's ancient history." History she hated to rehash so much she just couldn't bring herself to.

"Is it?"

"Yes." Jen pushed the plate back at Laurel. "Eat some of this, preggo."

Laurel grimaced and placed a hand to her stomach. "No. Eggs are an emphatic no right now."

Touched Laurel had made them for her even though she was feeling off about them, Jen gave in. All these twisting emotions were silly. "Ty and I had a secret thing back in high school. But that was forever ago." She wanted to say it had hardly mattered, but she knew she'd never make that lie sound like the truth.

"It seems like there's still—"

"No." Maybe things were still complicated, and maybe the *real* reason things hadn't worked out with Thomas was that because no matter how good-looking or funny or kind he was, he'd never made her feel the way Ty had—still did. But that didn't mean…

She didn't know what anything meant anymore.

"Do they know who wrote Ty those letters?" Because she could tell herself she didn't care, and that it was his problem, but the fact Ty Carson had called the police last night made her worry for him. It was so out of character he must be beyond concerned.

"No, and that's why I'm here. Jen, the last letter is in blood, and every letter points at someone who doesn't want to hurt Ty, but hurt the people he loves."

Though a cold chill had spread through her at the idea of a note written in blood, Jen attempted to keep her demeanor calm and unmoved. "He doesn't love me."

"Are you so sure about that?"

"Positive. He left. He made sure it was a clean break, and we're both different people now. Whatever feelings are between us are those weird old ones born out of nostalgia, not love. Of that I'm sure." She wanted to be sure.

"Okay, so maybe he doesn't still love you. But maybe whoever is threatening Ty thinks he does. From what Hart told me, Ty thinks it's someone from his army days, which points to someone who knew him when he still had a closer connection to you. It doesn't have to make sense to us, if we're dealing with someone who's deranged. And this stranger sniffing around your store is too much of a coincidence. You need to be careful until the police clear everything up."

Jen frowned. "Ty told me to stay at the ranch. I don't want to."

"As much as I'd usually support a contrary refusal to do anything a Carson ordered—"

Jen jumped to her feet and began to pace. "I'm not being contrary. I'm trying to be *sane*. If this man is really after Ty, and for some reason I'm his target, couldn't someone just tell him I don't mean anything to Ty? Wouldn't it be obvious?"

"So he can turn his attention to someone else? Grady? Vanessa? Noah and Addie and Seth?"

Jen closed her eyes against the wave of fear. "Laurel."

"I know it isn't fair, but the fact of the matter is, what we have to do is find out who this individual is and let the law handle them. Not try to shift his focus, much as I'd love it not to be on you."

Overwhelmed and feeling just a pinch sorry for herself, Jen sank back into the chair. "Why do bad things keep happening here?"

Laurel placed her hand over her slightly rounding stomach. "Maybe bad things need to happen to exorcise old feud demons. Maybe it's just bad luck of the draw, but at the end of every one of these 'bad things,' something really good has come out of it."

"I hope that's pregnancy brain talking because when I think of how badly you all have been hurt over the course of the past year—how many hospital visits I've made, how scared I've been—it isn't worth it."

Laurel reached over and squeezed her arm, still rubbing her stomach with her other hand. "It's been worth it to me. And we're all still here. You will be, too, but I want you to be careful, Jen. I want you to take some precautions. Whoever is behind this has left a lot of clues, has been careless, really. I'm hopeful it's all nipped in the bud before anything bad happens, but that means you watching your step and letting some people protect you until this person is caught."

Jen had worked very hard to never feel inferior to her siblings. They'd all always known exactly what they wanted to be, and had sacrificed to become it. Cam and his exemplary military service, and Laurel and her dedication to the law. Dylan and what they'd all thought was his education, but had turned out to be a secret military service of his own.

Jen had only ever wanted to run the store, and then once upon a time she'd wanted to risk everything for Ty Carson.

But it had never come to fruition and her life had been simple and exactly how she liked it. For ten years she'd had exactly what she'd wanted.

Except Ty.

"Why can't I protect myself every now and then?" Jen asked, not daring to meet her sister's gaze. "Why am I always the one who needs to be sheltered?"

"Because the people who love you are all licensed and trained to carry weapons. Because if there's anything the past year should teach us it's that working together and protecting each other is far better than trying to do it all alone. We're not asking you to hide in a corner while we fight your battles for you, Jen. We're asking you to let your family work *with* you to keep you safe during a dangerous time."

"I hate staying at the ranch."

"Join the club. Look, you can come stay with Grady and me, but…"

Jen wrinkled her nose. "He's asking Ty to come stay with you, isn't he?"

Laurel shrugged. "If it's all old news…"

"I'll stay at the ranch, but I'm still running my store. All my normal hours."

"Of course you are. We'll just want someone here with you while you do."

"Laurel."

Laurel pushed to her feet. "We'll come up with a schedule. You don't need to worry about that. Just be vigilant and don't go anywhere alone. That's all."

"That's all," Jen grumbled. "I enjoy being alone, Laurel."

"Well, for a little while you'll enjoy being safe instead." Laurel pulled Jen into a rare hug since she was not the touchy-feely type. "I have to get ready for work. Cam and Hilly are on Jen duty today. They'll just hang around your store being adorably in love. Give them a hard time about when they're going to get married. You'll have fun."

Jen grunted. "So what you meant by 'we'll figure out a schedule' is you already have."

Laurel ignored that statement and pointed to the eggs. "Eat that." She walked to the front door, all policewoman certainty.

"I wish I could be more like you," Jen muttered, not meaning for Laurel to catch it.

But she clearly did. She stopped in the doorway and turned to face Jen, her forehead lined with concern. "No you don't," she said forcefully. "You're exactly who you should be." Then she flashed a grin. "Besides, if you were more like me, you'd be married to a Carson, and no one wants that."

She left on a laugh, and Jen joined in, feeling somehow a little better for it.

"OVER MY DEAD BODY."

Grady rolled his eyes as he wiped down the scarred bar of Rightful Claim. "You're putting my bar in danger, cousin."

Ty didn't bother to roll his eyes right back. It was such bull he couldn't even pretend to get worked up about it. "I can handle myself, Grady. Lest you forget, I was an army ranger." Methodically, he kept pulling chairs off the tables and placing them on the floor.

"Lest you forget, two Carsons against a nut job are better than one."

"You've got a pregnant wife. Noah's got a wife and a kid at the ranch. I don't buy you're worried about your bar more than you're worried about that. Living here is the best place for me. Besides, it's all nothing."

Grady shook his head, clearly taking his irritation out on the bar. “My wife’s a cop and she—”

“Yeah, funny, that.”

Grady didn’t rise to that bait. “Laurel’s worried, which means I’m worried. You shouldn’t be sleeping in that apartment alone.”

Ty flashed a grin. “I’ll see what I can do.”

“Yeah, I’ll believe that once you’re able to look away from Jen Delaney long enough to hook up with someone.”

“Jen Delaney.” Ty made a dismissive noise, though his shoulders tensed against his will. “Sure.”

Grady clapped him on the back. “Lie to yourself all you want, Ty, but you aren’t fooling anyone. Probably including Jen. You’re coming home with me tonight, and that’s that.”

“You’re not my type.”

Grady just flashed him a grin. “Your type’s just changed, pal. Jen’s going to stay at the Delaney Ranch, against her will, and you’re going to be under Carson and cop surveillance against yours. Laurel thinks they’ll catch this guy in a few days. You can survive a few days in the presence of marital bliss.”

Ty knew Grady’s humorous tone wasn’t to be believed. His moves were jerky, and though he wore that easy grin, there was an edge to his gaze Ty knew better than to challenge.

At least until he found the *right* challenge.

Because he wasn't about to put Grady and Laurel in danger. Or Noah and Addie and Seth for that matter. It was good Jen would be staying out at the Delaney Ranch. Cam lived in the cabin on the property, and Dylan was currently residing in the house. Much as Ty didn't trust a Delaney as far as he could throw one, both men had been in the military and would protect their own.

Ty couldn't help thinking he'd do a better job of it, and all without bringing any innocent bystanders in. Not that Delaneys were ever really innocent, were they?

Jen is.

Hell. He worked with Grady in silence the rest of their opening routine. He manned the bar while Grady waited tables. The afternoon crowd was sparse, but it slowly got busier and busier as evening inched closer. Even a Monday night could have business booming, especially on a pretty day like today.

Autumn was threatening, and in Wyoming people knew to enjoy the last dregs of summer while they could.

Ty scanned the crowd, that old familiar *bad gut* feeling whispering over his skin. He recognized most of the patrons, but because of the historical atmosphere of the bar they often got strangers in from surrounding towns. It was unusual for him to know *everyone*.

But every stranger's face made him wonder, and every stranger's casual smile made him fear. He thought of all the real danger he'd faced as an army ranger and had never been jittery. Concerned on occasion, but never *nervous*. Determination and right and the mission before him had always given him a center of calm, of certainty.

But Jen had never been unwittingly tied to all those missions, and as much as he detested himself for being that weak, he knew it was the reason. Fear for *her*.

He had a terrible feeling whoever was doing this knew that, too.

His gaze landed on a stranger in a dark corner. All he could make out was a cowboy hat, pulled low.

Like the man on Jen's tape.

Ty forced himself to keep his gaze moving, keep his moves casual. He took the order of a usual customer, pulled the lever on the beer and glanced again at the man in the corner.

A flash of eye contact, and while he still felt no recognition to this man, he saw the *hate* in that gaze, and more damning, the flash of white-blond hair as Jen had described.

Fighting to keep his cool, and think clearly, he turned to give the beer to the person at the bar. When he quickly turned back to the stranger in the corner—he was gone, and the saloon doors were swinging.

Ty didn't think. Everything around him blanked except getting to that man. If he caught him, this would all be over.

He jumped the bar and ran, ignoring shouts of outrage over spilled beers and Grady's own concerned calling after him. Outside, Ty caught the flash of the man disappearing across the street.

Jen. Her store.

Ty ran as fast as he could, ignoring all else except catching the man who *had* to be responsible for all this. The stranger disappeared behind the buildings on Main, but since Ty had a feeling he knew where the man was running to, he kept his track on the boardwalk.

Once he got to the alley before Delaney General, he took a sharp turn and all but leaped into the back parking lot. Ty came to a stop, breathing hard, scanning the area around him, but there was nothing.

Nothing. With quick, efficient moves, Ty checked the back door. Locked and he hadn't heard a sound, so it was unlikely the man had beat him here and broken in.

He scanned the dark around him, but there was nothing, not even that gut feeling that warned him someone must be watching. He'd had to have run somewhere else. Ty could search but there were too many options. He could have even stashed a vehicle behind another business on Main and taken the back road out of town.

Ty cursed himself and he cursed the whole situation, but he also came to a conclusion.

He was going to have to do something even more drastic than getting the cops involved. Something no one would approve of, and something that could get him in quite a bit of trouble.

But Ty knew it was the only answer.

JEN HAD GOTTEN SURVEILLANCE. Bitterness ate through him like acid at the memory. How dare she protect herself against him and not Ty. She'd let that piece of trash into the back room of her store. Let him talk to her. She hadn't called the cops on Ty.

Red clouded his vision, and he had to be careful or the blood pounding in his ears would get too loud. Too insistent.

He concentrated on the steering wheel underneath his palms as he drove in a deliberate circle around Bent. He thought about Ty chasing after him and losing.

That made him smile. Yes, yes indeed. Ty wasn't nearly as fast as him, was he? Ty wasn't nearly as smart and strong and brave as he thought, was he?

The comfort at that thought lasted only a moment as he thought about earlier in the day. Jen and her surveillance. Anger came back, swift and addicting. He liked the way rage licked through his system, revved his mind.

Dr. Michaels said it was bad, but he didn't think so. He liked it too much for it to be bad. Didn't he deserve some of what he liked after everything he'd been through?

The man who'd been in Jen's store all day was clearly military, and he carried. He also touched Jen with far too much familiarity. The man guarding her would have to go on the list under the cop.

Yes, that would be good. Ty, the cop, the man in the store. Targets were good. The rage was good, but it had to have targets. Purpose. That's what Dr. Michaels didn't understand.

Maybe she'd go on the list, too. But not yet. Not now. First, he'd deal with the problems in Bent, Wyoming.

He drove down the back road behind the businesses on Main. He looked at the brick of Delaney General, the heavy steel door that would be tough to break into.

He'd have to make his move soon. He preferred to wait. Draw out the anticipation. Level out some of his rage lest he make a mistake.

But they weren't letting him, were they? And they'd be the ones who paid for his mistakes… so why not make a few?

Chapter Six

Jen had never felt particularly at home at the Delaney Ranch, though it was where she'd grown up. Unlike her brothers, she'd never been interested in the ranch work. She'd found the vast landscape unnerving rather than calming.

When she turned eighteen and moved into the apartment above the store, she'd been happier. She felt more herself there, like the building had simply been waiting for her. She liked to think it was the connection to her ancestors who'd run this store rather than raise cattle or protect the town with badge and honor. Like Laurel had always wanted to be a cop, Jen had always wanted her store.

So, waking up on the Delaney Ranch grated. But she did what she always did when she had to be here and didn't want to be—she made herself useful. It was the one thing that softened her feelings toward the place. Making meals or cleaning up. Laurel used to make fun of her "überdomesticity" but Jen found comfort in the tangible things she could do.

Surprisingly, Vanessa was the first person to enter the kitchen. Well, *stumble* was a better term for it. She was bleary-eyed, with messy hair, and she spoke only one word. "Coffee."

"Decaf?" Jen asked sweetly.

"Don't make me hurt you this early in the morning. I am allowed one cup of coffee per day and I will darn well take it."

Jen hid a smile and pulled down a mug. Though she knew Vanessa would just as soon do everything for herself, Jen didn't have any issue waiting on people. Especially pregnant people. "Sit," she ordered, pouring the coffee herself.

Vanessa lowered herself into a chair at the table and grasped the mug carefully when Jen set it in front of her. "Thanks. I don't suppose you're taking breakfast orders?"

"Only for pregnant women. The men around here get cold cereal as far as I'm concerned."

"Turns out I like you, Jen Delaney. I'm starving and the sound of everything makes my stomach turn."

Jen chatted with Vanessa over some possibilities until they came to something Vanessa thought she could stomach. Jen poured coffee for Dylan and then Dad when they arrived, but they both hurried out over some early meeting at the bank.

Dylan, of course, gave Jen a stern warning not to head to the store until Cam came over to escort her. She rolled her eyes at him, but then he kissed Vanessa's cheek and rested his hand on her belly and everything in Jen softened.

And sharp Vanessa Carson-Delaney softened, too.

"He'll be such a good dad," Jen said, more to herself than Vanessa.

"I'm counting on it. I don't have much in the way of good role models on the whole parenting thing." She shrugged philosophically. "Though I guess Dylan doesn't either."

Jen slid into the seat across from Vanessa with her own breakfast. "Doesn't it bother you, living here?"

"It's nice digs," Vanessa replied before taking a tentative bite of the oatmeal Jen had put together. "Apparently pregnancy has put your dad on his best behavior around me. Not much to complain about."

"Well, I'm glad, then."

"Gee, I think you mean that. Carsons and Delaneys might start holding hands and singing 'Kumbaya' before you know it."

Jen laughed. Even though it was ridiculous, the idea they were finding some common ground between their two families warmed her.

As long as she didn't think about Ty.

They ate breakfast companionably before Vanessa made her excuses to go take a shower and get ready for work. "Don't worry," Vanessa offered on her way out of the kitchen. "I won't leave till Cam gets here."

Jen huffed out a breath. She hated this babysitting. The stranger going after Ty, or her because of Ty, was hardly going to bust into the house and take her away. If he really was the stranger in her store, he'd already had ample opportunity to do that.

She cleaned up breakfast, glancing at her phone when it trilled. She frowned at the fact the text was from Ty of all people. Her frown turned into a scowl when she saw what he'd texted.

High Noon

It was their old code. Back in the days before they'd had cell phones, he'd simply leave a little note somewhere she'd see it, and that's all it would say for her to know to sneak out the back of the house and meet him at *their* tree.

She shoved the phone back on the counter. She was *not* responding to that. Not at all.

She focused on cleaning, and if occasionally she happened to crane her head toward the window, she stopped herself before she took a look toward the old gnarled tree in the backyard.

If Ty had something to say to her, he could come to the front door.

Her phone trilled again.

Come on, Jen. I need to talk to you.

Baloney. She wiped her hands off on a dish towel, then typed a response. Then talk.

I chased him last night.

She blinked down at those words, then swore. Oh, that man. Was he a moron? Did he have any sense of keeping *himself* safe? Chased him! And what him? Were they sure the note leaver and the man at her store were even the same person?

She shoved her phone into her pocket, then stalked to the front door. She yanked on boots, muttering the whole way. She marched out the front and around the back, a far cry from the teenager who would have snuck around, doing anything to avoid being seen by her family or the ranch hands.

She didn't care who saw her now, because

she was about to give Ty Carson a piece of her mind.

She stalked back to that old tree, determined to hold on to her anger and frustration, but the sight of him turned it to dust. His motorcycle was parked exactly where he always used to park it. Older and more lethal, he still looked windswept and she felt her heart do that long slow roll it had always done because Ty Carson was waiting for her.

Her.

She had to swallow at the lump that formed in her throat, embarrassed enough by the emotion to be irritated all over again. "We aren't in high school," she spat, terrified he'd read the rustiness in her voice as old longing.

If he did, he didn't comment on it. "No, we aren't, but I thought it'd get your attention."

She lifted her chin, wanting to feel lofty and above him. "It didn't."

"But me chasing after the guy did." He patted the motorcycle parked in the grass. "Hop on now. I need to talk to you about what happened. Privately."

"Is this yard not private enough?"

He tossed the helmet at her. She caught it out of reflex.

"Nope." He grinned. "Come on, Jen. You know you want to."

She did, God help her. She'd loved riding on the back of Ty's motorcycle in the middle of the night back in high school. It had been the most thrilling thing she'd ever done, aside from share herself with him. Ten years later and her life was staid. Boring. *Just the way you like it. You love your life.*

"Just up to the Carson cabin right quick, then I'll bring you back."

The fact he was so calm confused her. The fact she was tempted upset her. "They'll wonder where I am. They're worried enough."

"So tell them," he said, nodding toward the phone in her pocket. "This isn't cloak-and-dagger."

"Then why do we have to go somewhere else?"

Ty gave her a bland look. "You should really try to be more difficult, Jen. This back-and-forth is so much fun."

"I'm not getting on your motorcycle."

"All right. We can take your car."

She wanted to punch him, but it'd do about as much good as arguing with him. His body was as thick as his skull. "Fine. Just fine." She pulled her phone out and texted Cam and Vanessa that she was with Ty, and she'd let them know the minute she was back. Then she jerked the helmet onto her head and glared at him as she fastened it. "Let's get this over with."

She caught the boyish grin on his face, hated her body's shivering, *lustful* reaction to it. He swung his leg over the bike, waited for her to take her spot.

Your rightful spot.

She was making a mistake. She *knew* she was making a mistake, and yet she clambered onto the motorcycle just like she used to. She wrapped her arms around his waist just like she used to, and he walked the bike a ways down the hill until they were far enough away from the house for the roar of the engine not to reach anyone.

And *oh* the motorcycle roared and the wind whipped through her hair. She wanted to press her cheek to the leather at his back. She wanted to cry. It still felt like flying. It still felt *wonderful*. But she was old enough to understand it was having her arms around Ty, not the machine between her legs.

It was like traveling back in time, visiting with someone who'd died, knowing you'd have to go back to the living all too soon. She was too desperate for that feeling to let it go, even knowing pain awaited her on the other side.

He drove too fast, took turns too sharply, and

through it all she held on to him, biting her lip to keep from laughing into the wind.

When he reached the Carson cabin and cut the engine, it took her a moment to pull herself together and release him, then swing herself off the motorcycle. Took her far too many moments to wipe the grin off her face.

She sighed at the tiny clearing and the ramshackle cabin no one lived in but the Carson family used off and on. So many firsts in that cabin, though it had clearly had some repairs over the years. Uneasily, she remembered that last year Noah and Addie had fought off mobsters from Addie's past at this very place.

"Isn't it awful to be back here?"

Ty shrugged. "I don't care to remember Noah being shot, but he's all right now. Lots of shady crap happened here over the years. Such is life as a Carson. Besides, Addie's fixed it all up and they come up here. I figure they can take it, so can I."

She pulled off her helmet and hung it on the handle of the parked bike. "So, what did you want to talk about?"

His gaze was on the cabin, his expression… haunted. Was it what had happened to Noah here or was it that ride that felt like going back in time?

She didn't want to know.

"Let's go inside."

"Ty—"

He walked up to the door, pulling a key out of his pocket and ignoring all her protests.

She could ignore his demands. She could be petulant and wait outside and refuse to do any number of things.

But with a sigh, she followed him inside.

STEP ONE HAD been easy enough. Ty was a little surprised. Oh, he figured he still knew Jen well enough to press the right buttons, but it had all been so easy.

Now came the hard part. He had to get her phone off her. Once he had that, it'd be easy enough to keep her here. Safe and sound and under his supervision. There was the potential that someone would figure out where he'd taken her, but he had to hope they realized what he was doing was for Jen's safety.

And if they had to move elsewhere, well, he'd figure that out, too.

She'd probably consider it "kidnapping." He preferred to think of it as "safekeeping." She'd thank him eventually. Well, probably not ever to his face, but philosophically she might realize he did what was right.

Maybe.

Regardless, he *was* right. So, he had to go

about getting her phone off her. "Why don't you have a seat."

Eyebrows furrowed, she looked around the room. Addie's redecorating had made it look family friendly and inviting instead of what it used to be—a place to hide from the law or trouble.

Now it looked like a cozy cottage instead of an outlaw hideout. Ty couldn't say he liked the change, but with Noah and Grady all domesticated now, who was he to complain? They'd bring their kids up here and teach them to hunt, or have sleepovers with their cousins or second cousins. Make a nice little Carson-Delaney future on old Carson land. On old Delaney land.

Ty glanced at Jen, who'd taken a seat on the sky blue couch Addie had gotten to brighten up the living room. But Jen was the real thing that brightened the room. Her long, wispy brown hair and her pixie face, tawny brown eyes with flecks of green. She had a dainty, fairy-like quality to her and he felt like an oaf.

She looked so right there it hurt, like someone had shoved a knife right in his heart. He was halfway surprised to look down and see nothing there except his jacket.

Shoving his hands in his pockets, he ordered himself to focus. Get her phone away from her, and then keep her safe until the cops caught this lunatic. It'd be a few days, tops, he was almost sure of it.

If it was more, well, they'd reevaluate then.

He crossed to the couch, sat next to her. She raised an eyebrow at him, but he needed the proximity to get to her phone. So, he only smiled blandly in response.

Clearly irritated with him, Jen crossed her arms over her chest. "So, you have something to tell me that just had to be done in private?"

"Yes. The stranger that was in your store, he was at Rightful Claim last night."

Immediate concern softened her features, and he was momentarily distracted by all those things that had made him, of all people, fall for a Delaney in the first place.

Jen had been the softest, sweetest place he'd ever had the pleasure of landing. Growing up with an abusive father, she'd been like a balm. It hadn't mattered that she was a Delaney because she was kind. No matter how Grady or Noah had believed in the feud at the time—and wasn't that a laugh now?—Ty hadn't cared, because someone had loved him with a gentleness he'd never, ever had in his life.

Jen blinked, looked away as a soft blush stained her cheeks. Like she could read his thoughts, or had a few memories of her own.

"Jen—" But whatever ridiculous soft words

had bubbled up inside him, desperate to be free, were cut off by the way she looked at him.

Coolly. Detached, she returned his gaze. “You chased him. That’s what your text said.”

Business. All business. Good thing, too. Best decision he’d ever made had been to get the hell out of Jen Delaney’s life. No use playing back over what might have been, or even what still lurked between them. “Yeah. I thought he was heading for your store, but I lost him.”

“I stayed out at the ranch last night, so it wouldn’t have mattered.”

“It matters.” In a casual move, he rested his hand on the cushion between them—close enough his finger could gently nudge the phone farther out of her pocket.

She frowned down at his hand, but he kept it there as her gaze returned. He didn’t say anything because he was intent on inching his finger close enough to touch the phone that just barely peeked out of the pocket of her jeans.

“Why did you bring me here, Ty? What’s going on?”

He used his index finger to nudge the corner of her phone out of her pocket. If he could move it enough, get it at the right angle, it’d fall out once she stood up. Then he’d just have to hope she didn’t feel it or notice it for how long it would take him to secret it away.

So, he nudged and spoke. “The cops are on this whole thing, but I’m worried. I don’t like that this guy was hanging around your place and Rightful Claim. It feels off.”

“Laurel said he’s sloppy and they’ll get him in no time.” But no matter how brave she tried to sound, she chewed on her bottom lip. She shifted slightly, as if she’d felt the move of her phone.

Ty grabbed her hand before she could pat her pocket down. He’d done it out of desperation, but the sizzle of connection shocked him into forgetting all about the phone.

How did her hand fit with his, like a key to a lock? Even now that simple touch was all it took to make him forget his real purpose and remember her. The feel of her. The rightness of her. And how he’d been the one to mishandle it all, ruin it all.

She blinked once, as if coming out of the same dream, and then jerked her hand away. “What is this?” she demanded. She popped to her feet and he was relieved the phone fell right out, and she didn’t even notice. She paced as he scooted over and gently nudged the phone deep into the cushions.

Finally she whirled, as if she’d come to some grand determination. “It’s time to take me home.”

He smiled lazily, knowing it would make her narrow her eyes and curl her hands into fists. "About that."

"Tyler," she warned through clenched teeth.

It amazed him that he couldn't control his negative reaction to his full name when he'd spent a lifetime controlling any and all negative reactions he didn't want to broadcast. But he nearly flinched every time she leveled him with that haughty *Tyler*.

"We're not going anywhere. Not for a while."

She made a sound of outrage, then did exactly what he'd hoped. She stormed for the door.

He took the moment to fish her phone out of the couch and click off the sound before sliding it into the drawer of the coffee table. Even as she wrenched the front door open and stomped outside, he closed and locked the drawer before sauntering after her.

She stalked right over to his motorcycle and then kicked it over. She gave him a defiant look, but he refused to rise to the bait. Barely. No one, *no one* hurt his bike. But he'd give her a pass since he was…well, not kidnapping her.

Exactly.

"Very mature, Jen."

She flipped him off, which did give him enough of a jolt to laugh. He'd forgotten how much he enjoyed her rare flashes of temper.

"I'm calling Laurel. Do you really think—" She stopped as her hands patted every pocket of her jeans. Once, twice, before shoving her hands into each pocket.

She looked up at him with shock in her gaze. It quickly turned to murder as she let out a primal scream and lunged at him.

Chapter Seven

Jen couldn't ever remember being so angry. She wanted to take a chunk out of Ty. She wanted to bloody his nose or knee him in the crotch, and if she'd been able to see anything more than the red haze of anger, she might have been strategic enough to do any of those things. Maybe.

But she was too mad, stupid with it, and she launched herself at him, only to be caught and corralled. She landed precisely one punch to his rock-hard chest before he had his arms wrapped around her tight enough she couldn't wriggle her arms free.

She kicked, but he only lifted her off the ground, angling her so her kicks did nothing.

"I hate you," she spat, right in his face.

He only grinned. "Now, now, darling, your hellcat is showing."

She wriggled on an outraged growl, but he only clamped his arms around her tighter so she could barely move at all as he marched her back inside. So she was pressed against the hard wall of muscle that was the love of her life.

He'd brought her up here, stolen her phone and was thwarting all her attempts to unleash her anger.

"This is ridiculous. Insane. You've lost your mind. Do you really think my family won't come up here and—"

"No, I don't think they will," he replied, equitably, as he all too easily moved her to the living room.

She kept wriggling, but it was no use. He was very, *very* strong, and she refused to acknowledge the hot lick of heat that centered itself in her core.

He dumped her on the couch and when she popped to her feet, he nudged her back down, looming over her.

"Stay put."

"Or what?" she demanded, outrage at his behavior and her body's response boiling together into nothing but pure fury. "Going to stalk me? Leave me some threatening letters in blood? You're no better than—"

He all but shoved his face into hers, cutting off not just her words but also her breath. His eyes shone with that fierce battle light that had thrilled her once upon a time, and maybe it still did, though she didn't much feel like being honest with herself right now. She'd rather pretend the shaky feeling in her limbs was fear, not that old desire to soothe the outlaw in him. To love him until he softened.

"Don't compare me to the man doing this, Jen. Not now. Not ever. You may not like my methods, but I'm doing what I have to do to keep *you* safe."

Her heart jittered, and that pulsing heat she remembered so well spread through her belly like a sip of straight whiskey. But she forced herself to be calm, to be disdainful. "I'm only in danger because of you."

He pushed away from the couch then, but not before she caught the flash of hurt in his eyes. Why did it still hurt *her* to cause him pain? Why couldn't she be completely and utterly unaffected by him, his emotions, his muscles or that past they'd shared?

"Yeah, that's true, which is why it's my duty to protect you."

"I have a family full of dutiful protectors. I don't need you."

His back was to her, so she couldn't read how that statement might have affected him. He was silent for the longest time.

She should speak. Demand her phone back and demand to be taken home. Threaten and yell until she got her way.

But she knew how useless that was. A Carson had an idea in his head and she'd never be able to get through that thick skull. She'd have to be sneakier than that. More devious.

Sneaky and devious weren't exactly natural for her like they were for Ty, but hadn't she loved him and watched him for years? Didn't she know how to retreat, circumnavigate and end up with what she wanted?

And if she didn't know how to do that, she'd figure it out. He wasn't going to lock her up here in the Carson cabin like some sort of helpless princess.

Which meant she had to be calm and reasonable in response to his…his…idiocy.

"Ty," she began, her voice like that of a teacher instructing a student. "Be reasonable. You can't take my phone away from me, lock the doors and expect me to stay put. It isn't sensible, and I'm surprised at you. It isn't like you to act without thinking."

He turned to face her, appearing detached and vaguely, disdainfully amused. A trick of his she'd always envied.

"I've thought it through, darling. I know exactly what I'm doing. I was also quite aware you wouldn't like it."

Bristling, Jen curled her fingers into fists,

trying to center her frustration there instead of at him. "Laurel won't—"

"Laurel will. Because you'll be safe and out of harm's way, won't you?"

"Like Addie and Noah were?" she returned, knowing it would hit him where it hurt. No matter that she hated to hurt him, she was very aware she needed to.

"This guy isn't the mob," Ty replied, referring to the men who had hurt Noah and Addie here, but Ty had that blank look on his face that belied the emotion hidden underneath.

"You don't know who he is," Jen returned, gentling her tone without realizing it.

He was so *still*. The stillness that had once prompted her to soothe, to love. Because Ty's stillness wasn't the actual reaction. His stillness hid all the myriad reactions inside him. Ever since he'd been a boy she knew he'd developed that skill, a response to an abusive father, and she'd always seen his stillness for that little boy's hurt. She'd always ached over it.

God, she wished she no longer did, but it was there. Deep and painful. It was against every instinct she had to clamp her mouth shut and keep the soothing words inside.

"I can't figure out who he is when you're in danger. I can't *think* when I'm worried about you."

"I'm not your concern."

He scoffed audibly. "Oh, please."

"I haven't been for ten years. You didn't concern yourself with me when you disappeared without a goodbye. You didn't concern yourself with me for ten full years after you just..." It was bubbling up inside her, all the betrayal and the hurt she'd been hiding from him.

"You want to have that out now?" he asked, so cool and stoic it was like being stabbed.

Jen closed her eyes and pressed fingers to her temple. She had to find some semblance of control when it came to him. "No, I don't. It's ancient history."

"Maybe, but ancient history can fester and rot."

She opened her eyes, worked up her steeliest, most determined look. "Mine hasn't."

"Yeah. You and *Thomas* make a real cute couple."

Jen angled her chin. If he thought that, well, she'd use it. She'd use it to protect her heart. "We're very happy."

But his mouth quirked. "You haven't slept together."

Outraged, she stood. "You don't know that."

"Oh, I know it." He took a step toward her, but she would not back down.

She refused to be affected by the large man looming over her. He was not some romantic hero sweeping her off her feet. He was a thick-skulled caveman thinking he knew better than her and casting aspersions on her made-up relationship with a perfectly decent man.

However, she knew Ty well enough to know that arrogant grin meant he wanted a fight. She wouldn't give him one.

"I guess we'll have to agree to disagree," she said coolly. "Now, I'd appreciate my phone back. You can rest assured if my family agrees, I'll stay put."

"Because you're so good at doing what your family says?"

She smiled, trying to match his arrogance, though she was afraid it only read brittle. "I only made one very regrettable mistake in that regard. I learned never to make it again." She'd been hurt too deeply by the way he'd left her to ever, ever go back to a place where she'd give her whole heart so completely to someone.

She'd been stupid with youth and innocence, but she was older and wiser and she'd *learned.*

"Touché," he returned wryly.

"Now, perhaps we can have an adult conversation."

"I wouldn't count on it, darling."

She wouldn't let him get to her. He wanted to irritate her. He enjoyed it. So, she wouldn't give him the satisfaction. "Just what exactly is your plan? Surely you're aware you'll have to contact my family."

"Surely."

"As much sway as you have over Grady, it's highly unlikely he'll side with you over Laurel."

"Highly unlikely indeed," he returned, clearly mocking her.

Do not snap. Do not snap at this hardheaded moron. "So. What's the plan?"

"The plan is I tell your family we decided to get out of Dodge for a while, so to speak."

"They won't believe that."

He raised an eyebrow. "You came with me willingly, if you recall. What's not to believe?"

"That I didn't discuss it with them first."

Ty grinned at that. "Yeah, they'll have a real hard time believing we went off and did something without getting approval."

She waved a hand. "It's not like they know about us."

Ty blinked at that, some piece of that sentence piercing his impenetrable shell enough to show surprise. "What do you mean?"

"I mean no one knows what happened between us back then. Well, Laurel and I discussed it briefly the other day, but mostly no Delaney knows that there was ever an us, or that I ever did something without approval. They'd be shocked." She forced herself to laugh. "Can you imagine my father's reaction if he knew I'd been seeing you?"

Ty was too still, and not that stillness that covered up an emotional reaction. No, this was something more like a stillness born of horror. It didn't make any sense, and it made her heart pound too hard in her chest.

"Ty..."

He blinked and turned away. "I should call Grady. He'll believe me. We'll hide out here a few days, and if they still haven't caught the guy, we'll reevaluate."

"Ty—"

"I think Hilly will be able to run the store for you well enough. If not, your father will come up with someone. Consider it a vacation. Relax. Enjoy yourself. Take a bath or whatever it is women do."

"Ty," she snapped, vibrating now with unknown emotions, like a premonition. There was too much happening here and his evasion wasn't nearly as tidy as he'd clearly wanted it to be. Dread weighted her limbs, but she had to understand this. Even when her heart shied away from knowing. "Who knew?"

"Knew what? That I'd bring you he—"

"Tyler." She didn't snap this time. It was little more than a whisper, because she had this horrible, horrible weight in her gut she couldn't unload. "Who knew about us before?"

"It's a small town, Jen. I'm sure any number of—"

She stepped forward. While thoughts of violence whirled in her head, she merely placed her hand over his heart with a gentleness she didn't understand. It was hardly the first time her mind and heart were at odds when it came to Ty. "Tell me the truth."

He didn't look at her. He kept his gaze on the wall and his jaw clamped tight. She thought he was refusing to answer her, but as her hand fell from his chest, his throat moved.

"Jen, you said it was ancient history." But his voice was too soft, too gentle. Two things Ty almost never was—now or then.

But she had to know. She had to… There was too much she didn't know or understand and she needed this whole thing to make sense. If it made sense maybe she could lock all these feelings back in the past where they belonged. "And you said ancient history could fester and rot."

He looked down at her then, and it was like looking at the boy she'd loved. Strong and defiant in everything, but in the depth of those blue eyes she could see his storms and his hurts and his desperation to make things *right*.

It was what she'd always loved about him.

Then. Now? Her brain knew a person didn't still love someone after a ten-year absence, after the betrayal of leaving without a goodbye, and yet her heart...

"Your father knew."

It was a blow. It didn't matter and yet it felt like someone had plowed something into her stomach.

"He threatened you," Jen surmised, a light-headed queasiness replacing the pain. "That's why you left."

Ty laughed bitterly. "Sure, I was scared of the big bad Delaney. Get a grip, Jen. I left because I left."

She knew better, and it occurred to her now the reason she hadn't been able to get over Ty and her love for him was that she knew he hadn't abandoned her without a reason. He had a reason—one he didn't want her to know about.

It was ancient history, and she wanted to forget. But after he'd disappeared, she'd experienced grief as if he'd died, not just left.

Still, she didn't think he was lying, exactly. Ty had never been intimidated by her father. He'd never been scared of his reaction like she had been. She'd wanted to please her father, and she'd wanted to love Ty. She'd known both couldn't exist, so she'd kept them separate.

Or thought she had. Her father had known.

Ty had left because her father had known and—Oh, *God.* "He threatened me," she realized, aloud. "You left because he threatened *me.*"

"I would have joined the army no matter what." So still. So blank, and yet in his blankness she knew he felt a million things. In his blankness he confirmed her realization. He'd left only because of something Dad had done to threaten her life.

Ty hadn't left to save his own skin, or even simply because he'd wanted to. He'd left to protect her in some way. She wanted it to ease or heal something inside her, but it didn't. "You could have said goodbye."

"I have to call Grady. I have to—"

"What are you afraid of, Ty? That the truth from a decade ago will change something? I'm not so sure it will. The why of what you did doesn't change what you did, but maybe the truth would give us both some peace."

"Fine. You want truth and peace and moving on?" Temper sizzled, but he kept his hands jammed into his pockets. "Yeah, he threatened you. Said he'd sell the store if I didn't get the hell out and away from you. So, I did. You got your store, and I got the army, and life went the hell on." He jerked his shoulders in a violent shrug. "I figured he would have told you all that at some point."

Her store. Dad had threatened to sell her store. Jen sank onto the couch behind her. No, her father had never told her that. He wouldn't have, for one simple reason. "He wouldn't have sold the store. It was a bluff."

Ty raised a pitying eyebrow. "Sure, darling."

She wouldn't fall apart in front of Ty. Not when he was being so dismissive. Not when it proved what she'd always felt but tried to talk herself out of.

He hadn't left out of malice, or even to save his own skin. He'd left the way he had out of love. It changed nothing in the here and now, but somehow it changed her. Something deep inside her.

She didn't understand the shift, the feeling, but she figured with enough time she would. She glanced up at Ty, who looked like a storm encased in skin.

Time. They needed more time. So, she'd stay until the threat against her—against *them*—was gone. Then…

Well, then she'd figure out the next step.

THEY'D DISAPPEARED. A morning skulking around town and he hadn't seen hide nor hair. They'd tried to escape him.

It was nearly impossible to swim out of the black, bubbling anger threatening to drown him. But he couldn't let it win, because then he wouldn't succeed in his mission. In his revenge.

Using the prepaid phone he'd picked up at a gas station in Fremont, he dialed the old familiar number, trying to focus on the help he would find.

When the perky secretary answered, he tightened his grip on the phone. Some old memory was whispering something to him, but he couldn't understand it with the fury swamping him.

"I need to speak with Dr. Michaels."

There was a pause on the other end, and he snarled. He narrowly resisted bashing the phone against his steering wheel.

"I'm so sorry," the secretary said soothingly. It did nothing to soothe. "I thought we'd contacted all of her patients. Dr. Michaels will be off for quite a bit. We have a temporary—"

"I need to speak with Dr. Michaels. Now." He closed his eyes against the pain in his skull. It smelled like blood, and for a moment he remembered the singing joy of knocking the life out of that uppity doctor.

Hadn't that only been a dream?

Yes, just a dream, sneaking into her house and waiting for her to get home. Just a dream, standing in her closet and waiting for her to open it to hang up her coat.

Stab. Stab. Stab.

A dream.

The secretary was lying, that was all. Covering for her boss who was off *vacationing*. He'd put them both on the list.

On an oath, he hit End on the phone and threw it against the windshield. It thudded but didn't crack the glass like he'd hoped.

He needed to hurt something. Someone. Now.

But he wanted Ty. Jen. So maybe he'd just save up all the anger.

When he found them, they'd pay.

Chapter Eight

Ty didn't care for the tightness in his chest, but he wasn't about to let the woman sitting quietly at the small kitchen table see that. She'd already seen too much, disarming him with the gentle way she'd touched his heart and asked him to explain.

Who cared? So old man Delaney had told him he'd sell Jen's dream out from under her if Ty didn't disappear. So, Ty had listened. Didn't make him good or right. It was simply what had happened.

Why'd Jen have to bring it up? How had she not…known for all these years?

"You know, we have bigger fish to fry than our past," he snapped into the edgy silence they'd lapsed into while he'd put together some food for dinner.

"Yes, we do," she agreed easily. Too easily.

He shouldn't look at her. He knew what he'd see and what he'd feel, but he was helpless to resist a glance. Her expression was placid, reasonable even, but her hands were clasped tightly on the table and there was misery in her eyes.

He'd always known he'd bring her misery. He just hadn't known it would last so long.

"I'm going to call Grady. Tell him we're lying low for a few days."

She didn't look at him as she nodded. "Yes. All right."

She wasn't listening to him. She was lost in a past that didn't—couldn't—matter anymore.

He pulled his phone out of his pocket and dialed Grady's number as he walked into a bedroom. He stepped inside, closed the door and let the pained breath whoosh out of him.

What the hell did he think he was doing? Saving her? It wasn't his job or place. Maybe she was in danger because of him, but that didn't mean…

"You know Laurel's going to kill you, right?"

Ty might have laughed at his cousin's greeting if he didn't feel like he'd swallowed glass. "She should probably hear me out first."

"Good luck with that."

"Which is why I called you, not her," Ty said, keeping his voice steady and certain. "We're just going to lie low for a few days. Let the cops find the guy. Sensible plan if you ask me."

"Since when docs a Carson do the sensible thing and leave it to the cops?"

Ty wanted to be amused, but he was all raw edges and, if he was totally honest with himself, gaping wounds.

But wounds could heal. Would. Once this was all over.

"Your wife seems to have a handle on finding this guy," Ty explained. "Plus, a Delaney is in the line of fire, not me. Let Laurel and her little deputies figure out who this guy is and—"

"Who this guy is that's targeting *you*, Ty. Why aren't you trying to figure out who it is?"

The blow landed, and Ty refused to acknowledge it. "The cops have his DNA now. What am I supposed to do about it?"

"You've got the brain in your head, which I used to think was quite sharp. Now I'm wondering."

It hurt, and Ty would blame it on already being raw. "I don't know who it is. Not sure how I'm supposed to magically figure it out. I'm not a cop. Look. Jen and I will stay out of sight for a few days. Let the law work, much as it pains me. Safest bet all the way around."

"Then what?"

"What do you mean, then what? Then things go back the way they were and everyone's safe."

Grady was silent for too many humming

moments. "You can't run away every time you don't know what to do, or how to face what you have to do."

Shocked, knocked back as if the words had been a physical blow, Ty did everything he could to keep his voice low. "Are you calling me a coward?"

"No, Ty, I'm noticing a pattern. One you're better than." He sighed into the phone.

Ty searched for something nasty or dismissive to say, but Grady's words had hooks, barbs that took hold and tore him open.

"Stay out of town and keep Jen safe if that's what you have to do," Grady said, with enough doubt to have Ty bristling. "I'll convince my wife it isn't such a bad idea. I'll do that for you because I love you, but I think you're better than this. Maybe someday you'll figure that out."

Ty didn't have any earthly idea what to say to that, and he was someone who always knew what to say—even if it was a pithy comment designed to piss someone off.

In the end, he didn't have to say anything. Grady cut the connection and Ty was left in the small bedroom he'd snuck Jen off to for very different reasons their junior year of high school.

Grady didn't understand. He hadn't gotten out of Bent like Ty had. He didn't understand the world out there was different from their isolated little community in Wyoming. He didn't understand that sometimes a man had to get out and let someone else handle the aftermath.

Grady could think it was cowardice, but Ty knew it took a bigger man to do the right thing without concerning himself over his ego. Carsons ran on ego, and Ty had learned not to.

He'd keep Jen safe, and Grady might never understand, but Ty had never needed anyone's understanding. Ever.

Temper vibrated and he ruthlessly controlled it as he stepped back into the cabin's living area.

Jen sat in the same exact place at the kitchen table, looking at the same spot on the wall, fingers still laced together on the glossy wood Addie always kept clean. She'd barely eaten any of the canned chili he'd fixed earlier. She looked like a statue, regal and frozen and far too beautiful to touch without getting his dirty fingerprints all over her.

He shook that thought away. The days of loving her and feeling inferior to her were over. All that was left was keeping her safe from trouble he'd unwittingly brought to her door, and if he had to wade through some past ugly waters to do it, well, he'd survive.

"Grady'll handle Laurel."

Jen's all-too-pulled-together demeanor changed.

She looked over her shoulder at him and rolled her eyes. “Handle. You don’t have a clue.”

“So she’s got him wrapped up in her. Doesn’t mean he can’t handle her.”

“Do you pay attention at all? They work because they talk. They don’t agree on everything, they don’t handle each other, they *communicate*. And sometimes they still don’t agree, but they love each other anyway because if you actually try to understand someone else’s point of view, even if you don’t share it, you’re both a lot better off.”

“Is that some kind of lecture?”

She snorted. “God, you’re such a piece of work.”

He flashed his easy grin and didn’t understand why everything seemed to curdle in his stomach. “That’s what they all say, darling.”

She stood carefully, brushing imaginary wrinkles out of her shirt. “I want my phone back.”

“Afraid not.”

“I’ve agreed to stay with you. There’s no reason for you to keep my property from me.”

She’d never used that Delaney disdain on him. Not back then, and not even in the time since he’d been back now. Snarky sometimes, yes. Irritated, always. But not that cold, haughty voice as if she was a master talking to a servant.

He'd deal with a lot to keep her safe, to keep his own wounded emotions safe and locked away, but there was no way in hell he was putting up with that.

So he kept walking toward her, grinning the grin that made his soul feel black and shriveled. "Make me, darling."

JEN KNEW OF absolutely no one else who made her consider bodily harm on a person more than Ty. Being stuck in this cabin with him for even a few hours was already torture, and she'd shown admirable restraint if she did say so herself.

She would not lower herself to try to physically best him again. There was no point in a shouting match or demanding her phone back. So, she'd take a page out of her father's notebook and play the better-than-thou Delaney.

She didn't *feel* better than anyone, but she supposed that didn't really matter.

"Fine, if you want to play your childish games, keep my phone." She shrugged as if it was of no consequence. "We're not going to sit around here like lumps on logs," she decided. "We're going to do our own detective work. We'll start with a list of people who would have reason to threaten you, and me through you.

You'll need to get a piece of paper and a pen so we can write it all down."

"You're not very good at the lady of the manor crap. You'll have to practice."

She raised an eyebrow at him and knew her face didn't betray a flicker of irritation or hurt. "Lucky for me, I have all the time in the world to do so."

He held her gaze for a long time. Too long to win the staring match. Still, she thought the move to get situated on the couch in the most dismissive manner she could manage was a good enough substitute to staring him down.

Then she simply waited, fixing him with a bland stare of expectation. His jaw worked before he finally gave in and walked over to the kitchen silently. He jerked open a few drawers before pulling out a pad of paper and a pen.

"Thank my sister-in-law for these homey little touches." He returned, dropping the paper and pen on the coffee table in front of her.

"I like Addie," Jen returned.

"She's a Delaney, so I don't know why you wouldn't."

"She makes Noah happy," Jen persisted, wanting *something* to get through that hard shell of his. "She and Seth make Noah as happy as I've ever seen him."

"Your point?"

"Maybe *you* should thank Addie for the homey touches without being so derisive."

He held her gaze, but nothing changed in his expression. "You wanted to make a list?" he said, just the tiniest hint of irritation edging his tone.

She picked up the paper and the pen, because she did want to do this and there was no need to belabor points about love and happiness in this little hell she found herself in. She poised pen on paper and ignored the way her heart hitched. "I suppose my father would be on the list."

Ty heaved out a sigh. "It ain't your father."

"No, it seems unlikely," Jen agreed, doing everything to sound calm and polite. "But we're starting from nothing, which means no stone left unturned. My father dislikes you. He's threatened me to get to you before apparently. He fits."

"He's not the man who's been skulking around your store or my saloon."

"No. He isn't. But that man could be working for my father. It's not out of the realm of possibility."

Ty didn't argue with that, but he paced the small living room area. "I don't recognize him. If he was someone I'd known, someone who knew *me* personally, wouldn't I recognize him? In your tape. In Rightful Claim. There'd be *some* recognition."

She could see the fact he didn't know the man bothered him on a deeper level than she'd originally thought. The fact there was even the smallest ounce of helplessness inside him softened her. She wanted to reach out and touch his hand, something gentle and friendly and reassuring. She even lifted her hand, but then she let it drop back onto her thigh.

"It's not unheard of for someone to pay someone else to enact some sort of revenge or whatever this is."

Ty shook his head. "I saw him, Jen. There in Rightful Claim. He hated me. I saw it on his face. He *hated* me. But I don't know who he is."

She stayed quiet for a few humming seconds, reminding herself it wasn't her job to comfort him. She was angry with him and she would give him no solace in this, no matter how impotent he felt—not something a man like Ty Carson was used to.

Not her problem, and *not* something she was going to care about. "You don't recognize him, but he hates you. So, who hates you? If you just start naming people it might dislodge a memory. It's also possible this man is connected to someone on the list. Sitting here waiting for Laurel to figure it out—"

"I'd settle for any half-brained cop to figure it out, or a lab to get DNA on that blood."

"I'm sure they'd settle for that, too," Jen replied primly. She wanted to defend Laurel, considering her older sister was the strongest, smartest, most dedicated person Jen knew, but it would land against that hard head like a peaceful breeze and fall on deaf ears. "For now, we write a list." She smiled sweetly over at him. "Even if the police figure it out first, you'll have a handy reference for the next time someone tries to..." She trailed off and frowned.

This person wasn't trying to hurt Ty—not physically. The person who wrote the notes, if he was the same person stalking her store, wanted to cause fear. Worry—not for Ty's own welfare, but for hers.

"They don't want to hurt you—they want to cause you pain," Jen muttered, working through the problem aloud.

"I think that's the same thing, darling."

"No. No, it isn't. If they hated you, they'd want to hurt you."

"He *does* hate me, that's what I'm saying."

She waved him away, trying to think and connect the dots she was so close to connecting. "This person you don't recognize hates *you*, but wants to hurt someone he thinks you l-love." She tripped over that l-word a bit, but she hurried past it and didn't look at him. "So, it would make sense that you didn't hurt this individual. You hurt someone *he* loved."

"You really want a list of all the women I've hurt, Jen?"

"It doesn't have to be a woman, Ty. There are lots of different kinds of love. But yes, if you hurt someone enough that they hated you—that someone who loved them might have hated you—then we should put it on the list. Again, my father qualifies."

"It's not your father."

Jen couldn't see it either, but it fascinated her that Ty was so insistent. Ty, who'd always hated her father, and surely still did. But he refused to consider her father might be behind this.

So, she kept poking at it. "Then who is it?"

Ty shook his head, but in his next breath he started naming names, and Jen went to work to write them down.

WITH THE POLICE SCANNER, the cops were easy to thwart. They only had three on duty in the area at any given time, so he always knew where they were or where they were headed.

The detective was a little bit harder to track,

but knowing she was sister to Jen and married to one of Ty's relatives gave him some intel.

He'd followed the detective around a bit in the afternoon on foot. She'd been in her patrol car, but the town was small, and with his radio she was easy to find.

To watch.

To wait.

She looked like Jen. She might do as a substitute. He'd hurt her just a little. Just a little. It'd take the edge off.

He considered it as he got back in his car when he realized her shift was over. He followed, taking a few turns out of her line of sight so she didn't suspect anything. When she turned off the highway, he parked his car along the shoulder. He slapped one of the abandoned-vehicle tags he'd stolen weeks ago on the back window so no one would think twice about his car being there.

Then he walked up the lane, and to the gleaming-new-looking cabin in a little cove of rock and trees. She was pulling things out of the trunk of her police car.

He could do it. Hurt her. Kill her. Spill blood. Right here, right now. She wore a gun, but what were the chances she'd have the reflexes to hurt him first?

Keep your focus. Keep your focus.

Dr. Michaels told him he did better with a goal. And his goal was causing as much emotional and *then* physical harm to Ty Carson as possible. The cop would be a distraction.

But he ached with the need to kill, and Jen's sister was ripe for the killing.

A loud engine sound cut through the quiet, and the cop shouldered her bag and shaded her eyes against the setting sun. A man roared up on a motorcycle. Not Ty as he'd hoped, but the other one. Not the brother, but a cousin, maybe.

People who mattered to Ty. It would be Ty's fault if they were harmed or killed. Ty would have all that guilt, and his would be gone.

He could pick them off in quick succession—bam, bam—and they'd fall to the ground. He wanted it. Needed it. His hand even reached for his side, but he remembered when he came up with nothing that he'd purposefully left his pistol in his car.

"Ty's the target," he whispered, reminding himself this was premature. Have a goal, Dr. Michaels had always told him. He ignored the tears of rage and disappointment streaming down his cheeks.

The goal was Ty, not these people. Jen was the best target. A decision he hadn't made lightly.

He'd do everything he wanted to do to Jen

and more, maybe in front of Ty himself. Yes, Ty had secreted her away, but he'd find them.

He'd find them and they would know true pain, and Ty would know true guilt.

And him? He'd finally be at peace.

Chapter Nine

The world was black and she couldn't breathe. Jen tried to thrash, but her body wouldn't move. She saw blood, smelled it even. But it wasn't her blood. It bathed the floor around her, but she wasn't hurt. So who was?

She sat bolt upright, eyes flying wide, her sister's name on her lips.

But Laurel wasn't in this unfamiliar room with her. There was no blood. Only slabs of wood, bathed gold in the faint light of a lamp on the bedside table.

Jen wasn't alone, though. No Laurel, no blood. She was in a comfortable bed, heart beating so loud she couldn't hear the horrible sound of her ragged breathing. "Ty?"

Still not fully awake, she reached for him, found his hand warm and strong. Something inside her eased, the sharp claws of panic slowly receding with the contact. Ty was holding her hand and she was safe.

"You were dreaming." His voice was flat, but he was there. When they'd decided to call it a night, he'd gone into one bedroom and she'd gone into another. But just now she'd been in the middle of a horrible nightmare she couldn't seem to fully shake, and he was here in this room with her.

Holding her hand.

"Breathe," he ordered, but there was no snap to his tone. A tinge of desperation, but nothing harsh.

So, she sucked in a breath and let it out. She squeezed his hand because it was her anchor. "It was Laurel. She was hurt."

"Laurel is fine."

"I know. It was just a dream." She fisted her free hand to her heart. "It just felt real. So horribly real. I could smell it."

"Just keep breathing."

So she did. She looked around the room, trying to orient herself. The Carson cabin. It looked so different from when they'd been in high school and snuck up here to…

Well, it wouldn't do to think of that, or how good it would feel to curl up into Ty's strong, comforting body and—

Yeah, no. She focused on the room. It was different from how it had been. New furniture, new curtains. Definitely new linens on the bed, and a pretty area rug that softened the harsh wood walls that had stood for over a century.

It smelled the same, though. The slight must of old not-often-used house and laundry detergent. She blinked owlishly at the lamplight, then at Ty.

He was rumpled, and still. So very still, perched on the edge of that bed like she might bite. But his hand held hers.

It would have amused her, if it didn't make her unbearably sad.

"Good?" he asked abruptly.

She nodded and he withdrew his hand and got to his feet. He shoved his hands into the pockets of his sweatpants and refused to meet her gaze. "Need anything?"

She did, but she didn't know what exactly. Surely not whatever he was offering, or rather, hoping she wouldn't take him up on.

She rubbed her hand over her chest. She'd calmed her breathing and her mind, but she felt clammy and shaken. There'd been so much blood, and it had been real enough to smell it, to feel it.

It was worse, worrying for someone you loved. So much worse than being concerned over your own safety. But it had been only a dream. Laurel was safe and sound at home, with Grady. Jen hadn't had any silly danger dreams last year when Laurel had been facing down *real* danger, so it was foolish to believe her dreams were suddenly premonitions.

"Jen. Do you need anything?"

She shook her head, trying to focus. "No. No, I'm all right." Which wasn't true. At all.

Ty moved swiftly for the door, and that made all the ways she wasn't all right twine together into panic.

"No, that's a lie. I'm not all right. I'm afraid."

He paused at the door. He didn't turn, but he stopped. "Fear's natural," he said quietly, surprising her.

She rarely told anyone in her family when she was afraid. She'd learned at a young age Delaneys weren't supposed to be afraid. They were supposed to *endure*. And if not, she was the weak one to be protected.

Hadn't that been the appeal of Ty Carson? He hadn't treated her like a fragile little girl, or like she was a little beneath him. He'd been curt with her, rough at times, and she'd known, deep down, he'd thought she was a little better than him.

It wasn't true, but she'd known he'd felt that way, and part of her had relished that. A painful thing to realize, to admit to herself. But she'd been a teenager. Didn't she get to cut herself some slack?

Shouldn't she cut *him* some? "You're not going to tell me not to worry about it, that you'll handle it and I'm just fine?"

"No."

She picked at the coverlet over her legs. She knew he didn't want to have this conversation, to listen to her insecurities, but she also knew he would. And she'd feel better for it. "Everyone else does."

"Everyone else… Listen…" He turned to face her, hands still shoved deep in his pockets and a scowl on his face. He looked like he was preparing for a brawl, but she knew that was always how he looked when faced with a conversation he felt like he needed to have even though he didn't want to. "I've been in a lot of real dangerous situations, and a lot that only *felt* dangerous. Nothing I did could erase the fear whether the danger was real or perceived. You learn to hone it. You should be afraid. What's going on is scary."

She wrapped her arms around herself, trying to hold those words to her heart. "As pep talks go, that was surprisingly effective."

"It isn't always the fear that gets us, it's the idea we can't or shouldn't be afraid. Fear is natural. To fear is to be human."

Human. Such a complex idea she never really considered. In her memories of Ty he was either that perfcct paragon of nostalgic first love, or he was the symbol of the way he'd left her. The way she'd thought about him since he'd been back had been one-dimensional. It had been about *her* feelings, and nothing to do with him as a human being.

It wasn't wrong, exactly. It was just more complicated than that. He was human. She was human. Fears, confusions, mistakes.

Whoever was trying to hurt them was human, too, underneath whatever warped thing made a person want to hurt someone. Human and hurting and doing terrible things to alleviate the hurt.

She didn't want that to be her. She'd done no terrible things, but she'd shoved herself farther and farther into a box without ever dealing with the here and now. The feelings that hurt and diminished all that she was.

It was time to stop. "I don't really want to be alone." She didn't admit things like that. She'd never had to. She'd never had to ask for what she wanted or needed—she either got it easily or she kept that want locked away until she forgot about it or learned to live without it.

She'd thought that was being adaptable, learning to live without what life refused to give her. But sitting here in this bed that wasn't hers, a man who wasn't hers lurking by the door, fear and confusion and hurt lying heavy on her heart, she had to wonder.

Was never asking for the things she wanted holding her back? Is that what had kept her comparing every man she'd ever dated with the man of her high school dreams? A fear of asking for more—for what she wanted—for anything.

"Could you stay?" They might have been the scariest words she'd ever voiced. They opened up every fear of rejection she'd ever harbored without fully realizing it.

But if she could live without the thing when she didn't ask, why not be able to live with it when she did? It was the same. Living without was all the same. If she asked, though, she might get something.

Ty eased himself onto the corner of the bed, still keeping a large distance between them. Because he didn't want to be here. He didn't want to stay with her, but she'd asked.

She'd asked, and he stayed.

WHEN TY WOKE up to the ringing of his phone, he was stiff and disoriented. A mix of familiar and unfamiliar assaulting his senses. The smell of the cabin, mixed with something fruity. The familiar warmth of the sunlight on his face that always snuck through the crack in the curtains, the unfamiliar warmth of a body next to him.

Thc phone stopped, and groggily he tried to figure out why he should care. Jen shifted next to him, and when he looked down on her—a completely ill-advised move—her eyes blinked open.

A deep brown with flecks of green that reminded him of the woods they used to sneak off into. That reminded him of the plans he'd let die because he'd been young and stupid. Because for all his ego and bluster, he'd believed, deep down, he wasn't fit to touch her.

As she held his gaze, sleepy but probing, he wasn't sure if he still believed that. Fear was human, he'd said last night. And people were human. No better or worse for their name or their mistakes. Just…human.

Maybe there was something here to…

"Thank you."

Thank God for those two words. It broke the spell. *Thank you* disgusted him enough to swing off the bed. "For what?" he grumbled, already heading for the door. He wanted her gratitude as much as he wanted another hole in the head.

"For staying," she replied simply.

His eyes were on the door, on exit and escape, but the vision of that dark forest that had been theirs haunted him, that little seed of a thought that things could be different now. As adults. "You were scared, and it was my fault," he said disgustedly.

"Yes. Of course. It could have only been done out of guilt."

Surprised, he turned on her. "What other reason would I have?"

She held his gaze, but then shook her head and yawned. She slid out of bed, shuffling toward the door. "I need coffee for this."

Remembering how annoyingly chipper she got after her first cup in her, he lied. "We never have any coffee at the cabin."

She whirled on him so fast, so violently, he actually moved back a step, afraid she was going to punch him.

He held up his hands in surrender, amused in spite of himself. "That was a joke, darling."

Her eyes narrowed, those dainty fingers curling into fists. "Not. Funny." Then she whirled back around and sailed out of the room.

"It was a little funny," he murmured to himself. He made a move to follow her, since he could use a jolt of caffeine himself. Before he managed to move, his phone rang again.

Frowning, he crossed the room and grabbed it off the nightstand. He didn't recognize the number, so he answered it cautiously.

"Yeah?"

"Would it kill you to answer your phone on

the first call?" He recognized Laurel's irritated voice immediately. She must have been calling from the police station.

He sneered a little at that. "What do you want, Deputy?"

"I want to talk to my sister, but first I need to talk to both of you. Speaker on."

Ty strolled into the living room. "I ain't one of your deputies you get to boss around, Laurel."

"No, but I am your cousin-in-law, the detective in charge of this investigation and the woman who could charge you with kidnapping if you don't do what I say."

"I—"

"But beyond all that, Carson. I've got a name for your guy. So, why don't you cooperate so we can actually talk this out."

He wanted to find a comeback for that. A way to defend that kidnapping charge and pretend the rest didn't matter. But a name mattered. "Fine," he ground out, hitting Speaker on his phone and slapping it against the kitchen table.

"Jen? You're all right?"

"Yes," Jen replied, leaning closer to the phone. "I didn't realize Ty was talking to you, but I suppose I should have with all the bickering. How on earth do you and Grady get along?" Jen wondered, looking longingly at the slow-dripping coffee machine. "Your natural bossiness and his natural Carson-ness."

"Somehow it works," Laurel replied. She was in *all*-cop mode right now—even over the phone—and didn't rise to Jen's sisterly teasing bait. "I've got a missing person who matches the description of the man that was in Rightful Claim and what we could see of the customer who fainted on Jen's store tape."

"The blood?" Ty demanded.

"Still waiting on the results, but we have a name to confirm against, so that's a step. The next step—"

"What's the name?"

"The next step will be—"

"I want his name."

Jen placed her hand on his forearm, and it was only then he realized his entire body had hardened, and that he was all but ready to punch a phone. Worse, that her simple touch did ease some of the tension inside him.

"Laurel. Ty just wants to know if he recognizes the name. Let's start with that, then go through all the steps."

"His name is Braxton Lynn. It's not a perfect match since we don't have a clear picture of him, but it's close enough to wonder."

All the tenseness inside Ty leaked out fully, and futility swept in heavily and depressingly in its wake. "I don't know that name." A dead end. No matter how he went through his memory, the name Braxton *or* Lynn didn't ring any bells whatsoever. Someone was after him, ready to hurt the people he…cared for, and he didn't know the face *or* the name.

"Apparently he's from Phoenix, Arizona," Laurel continued. "I've got some calls in with a couple PDs in the area to get more information on him, maybe get a more positive ID. Criminal record on the Braxton name appears clear from what I've been able to search, but he's been missing for three months. Adult, twenty-six, no family looking for him. A foster sister reported the missing person, but it doesn't seem like anyone's too eager or worried to find him."

"I don't know that name," Ty repeated irritably.

"But we discussed something last night that I think is pertinent," Jen interrupted, sounding so equitable he wanted to growl. "Whoever is here might be threatening Ty or me because of a perceived hurt on a loved one. This Braxton might have a family member or friend who *does* have a connection to Ty."

"It's a solid theory," Laurel said, considering it. But then she barreled on, pure cop. "Like I said, I've got calls in trying to get some more background. Since this is all desk work, I'll handle trying to track down more of a profile and I'll keep you both updated. What about Phoenix?"

"What about it?" Ty retorted, repeating the name in his head like an incantation. *Braxton Lynn. Braxton Lynn.* Why didn't he know that name?

"You don't know the name," Laurel said as if it wasn't a failure on his part. "But what about anyone from the area? If it's a connection we're looking for, maybe it's Phoenix."

Ty stomped away from the phone on the table and paced, raking his hands through his hair. Phoenix? Not that he could think of, but Arizona...maybe. Maybe?

He moved back to the table, leaned close enough to talk into the speaker. "I had a buddy back in the army, before I became a ranger." One who'd had reason to hate him, but how could a kid from Phoenix be connected to a soldier from a small town? "Oscar Villanueva. I can't see as how there'd be any connection, but he was from Arizona. Not Phoenix, though. Some place I'd never heard of and can't remember now."

"Okay. You got any contact information for Oscar?"

Just another failure. "No," Ty managed to say, still sounding pissed instead of broken.

"No. We lost touch when I got into the rangers." He didn't mention why Oscar might hate him. It wasn't pertinent until they found a connection.

"Okay. I'll dig into that angle. If you think of the name of the town, you let me know. I find any more connections or the blood results come in, I'll give you a call."

"Yeah," Ty returned, gut churning with emotions that would get in the way of clearheaded thinking. He needed all this…stuff inside him out of the way. He needed to compartmentalize like he had back in the army.

Tie it up. Set it aside. Act on fact and order over *feelings*.

"Take care of my sister, Carson, or you'll have a lot more than me to answer to."

Ty scowled at his phone. "She'll take care of herself." He hit End without waiting to hear what Laurel had to say about that.

Jen sighed. "Ty. You shouldn't have said that."

"Why not?" he returned. "You can and do take care of yourself."

He wanted to pace, to expend the frustrated energy inside him, but pacing was wasted. Maybe he'd go lock himself in the bedroom and do as many push-ups and sit-ups as it took to clear his mind.

"Yes, but you know how Laurel worries. How my family worries. You just added to it by—"

"They should get a new hobby, and so should you for that matter. It isn't your job to placate them."

She didn't bristle like he'd thought she would. She moved to the coffeemaker, unerringly finding the right cupboard for the coffee mugs. "It's been a rough year," she said, and though she sounded unshakable, there was a sadness to those words.

But she hardly had the monopoly on hard years. The Carsons had been through their fair share of what the Delaneys had gone through—though a few more Delaneys had landed themselves in the hospital. Carsons, too, though, so... "For mine, too, darling."

"I don't want to fight with you, Ty." She took a sip of coffee, winced, presumably at the heat. "I want to figure this out so I can go home to my store and live my life."

"Funny, I thought we could do that *and* bicker."

Her mouth almost curved, but the sadness remained. "We can, but I don't want to." She held out a hand. "Truce?"

He didn't want to touch her. There'd been too much already, and his brain had taken a few more detours than he cared for. But the less she knew about all that, the better. "Fine. Truce." He shook her hand.

The chill that skittered up his spine had nothing to do with the handshake. He frowned, looking at the door. He wasn't sure what the feeling was, the foreboding signal that something was off.

"I feel it, too," Jen whispered. "What is it?"

"It's your gut," Ty replied, eyeing every possible entrance in the cabin. Not too many windows, but enough. The door would be impossible to penetrate. The secret passageway had been bolted shut after Addie'd had to use it last year.

"My gut says we should get a gun," Jen said, still holding his hand in hers.

"Yeah, your gut ain't half-bad."

IT HAD BEEN easy to track the motorcycle marks once he'd found them. It had taken him longer than he'd wanted to finally discover the trail, but the Delaney Ranch was rather hard to breach even with all its stretching fields and nooks and crannies.

Good security there, plus a parcel of ranch hands always roaming about and a passel of vigilante residents. He'd nearly gotten himself caught three times.

But now, *now* he was following the heavy

divot in the grass clearly made when a motorcycle had irresponsibly driven up the east side of the property, and then driven off again on dirt roads.

Irresponsible Ty. Always making mistakes. Including driving up the unpaved road, rather than turning back to the highway.

He could track the land—especially since the sun had seemed to bake the tracks in good, different from the truck tires that also marred the dirt.

He clucked his tongue at Ty's idiocy. Such a shame Ty would make it so easy for him. The laugh bubbled into his throat, escaped and echoed through the trees. He rather liked the sound of it, but he should be more careful. He wouldn't make a stupid mistake like Ty had.

No. Mistakes wouldn't bring him peace or closure. Mistakes weren't his goal. So, he climbed, following the motorcycle track up and up and up.

He was starting to get winded as morning began to dawn in earnest. Mist that had filtered through the trees began to burn off.

The higher he got, the more the trees thickened, but the road remained. Ty's careless tire tracks guiding him. What utter stupidity.

Jen was better off with him, not Ty. She'd see that eventually. She'd be his prize. Oh, he'd have to hurt her to hurt Ty, but she'd understand. Once she knew the whole story, she'd understand. They could build a life together. Because he'd have peace then. Peace and closure.

Hurt Jen. Kill Ty. Live happily ever after?

It wasn't the plan. Dr. Michaels told him he did better with a plan. With a goal. But couldn't plans and goals change? Didn't he deserve a prize? Jen didn't deserve to die.

But she'd run away from him. She'd called the cops on him. She was *with* Ty. Clearly, she needed to be punished. Like Dr. Michaels, who hadn't listened—not close enough.

So, perhaps it would be up to Jen herself. Defend Ty? Die. Let Ty touch her? Die more painfully. He could envision it. The glint of the knife. The smell of the blood. Just like the uppity doctor.

No, no, that had been only a dream. Maybe he'd dream about Jen, too. Dream about her begging for Ty to save her, but he wouldn't. Ty wouldn't be able to. Ty would have to watch her die. Slowly.

He could see it and he needed it. Now. He needed the kill now. Murder sang its siren song. It flowed through his blood. He could *feel* it there, boiling inside him. It needed release. Knife to throat.

He had his knife out in his hand. Maybe he'd use it on himself. Just a little bit. Just to take the edge off.

Then he saw the cabin.

Chapter Ten

Jen watched Ty sweep the cabin with military precision. It didn't seem to matter that they hadn't heard anything, that it had been only this cold chill of a feeling that had gone through both of them. Ty was behaving like they were in imminent danger.

Surely it was just coincidence or…something. It unnerved her more than the feeling itself that he'd felt it, too, and that he took it seriously.

People didn't just *feel* things. If they did, her dream last night about Laurel was a lot more ominous. But Laurel had called this morning with a lead and everything had been fine.

Everything *was* fine, because Ty found nothing. He was now perched in what appeared to be an uncomfortable position, looking through the slight gap in the curtain at the front of the cabin.

"Ty, this is silly. There's nothing out there. We're both wired and worried."

"We both felt something," Ty returned, as if

that was just a normal thing people experienced. As if a shared feeling of discomfort or unease magically meant someone was out there.

"But that doesn't make any sense, Ty. It can't be possible."

He shrugged, his gaze never leaving the small patch of yard. "In the rangers you learn to roll with the things that don't make sense. It's not like *we* ever made any sense."

"Why not?" she asked before she remembered that this constant mix-up of them and this situation was only going to cause more heartache. She'd had her epiphany last night about asking for what she wanted, but what about things she didn't know if she wanted?

Part of her wanted Ty, but she didn't think it was a very intelligent part of herself.

Ty scoffed at her question. "Aside from the fact we're opposite in just about every way—a Carson and a Delaney. Ring any cursed bells?"

"That's not holding much weight these days."

"That's these days. Besides, we're still opposites."

"And opposites attract."

Ty shook his head, but his gaze was outside and his demeanor was completely unreadable. "There's got to be some common ground for all those differences to rest on. Attraction is easy."

She didn't know why she felt the need to

argue with him, only that she did. It made what they'd had before seem…doomed. An unimportant castoff.

It wasn't that. She wouldn't *let* it be that to him. "Then how do you explain Laurel and Grady?"

"Aside from the fact they both love and would protect the people they love with their life, they love Bent. They believe in it. Honestly, deep down, Laurel and Grady have more alike things than different."

Even knowing it was true, even having said the same to her brother Dylan in defending Grady and Laurel—back before he himself had been felled by a Carson—it irked her that Ty of all people recognized it.

"All right. Explain Dylan and Vanessa."

"Again, they might antagonize each other, but it's only because they're so alike deep down. They want the world to see the persona they put forth, not who they actually are."

It had taken her *years* to understand that about Dylan, and Ty said it like it was common knowledge.

But there was one truth he was refusing to acknowledge, and since he was irritating her with his truths, she'd irritate him with hers. "We're the same deep down, too."

He snorted. "I don't think so, darling."

"You don't have to. I know so. You've only ever tried to harden yourself against that gaping need for someone to love and cherish you and let you protect them, and I've hidden myself against the very same thing."

She watched those words land—that stillness, then the slight rotation of shoulders as if he was willing the words to roll off his back.

But truths weren't easy to shrug away. That she knew.

Then everything in him stiffened, and he brought the binoculars he held in one hand to his eyes.

"Don't pretend you see something just to get out of—"

"There. He's out there."

She rolled her eyes and fisted her hands on her hips. She was not this stupid, and it was insulting he thought she was. "You are not going to change the subject by—"

He thrust the binoculars at her. "He's out there."

Frowning at the binoculars, Jen took them hesitantly. "How do you know it's him?"

"Movement."

"It could be an animal," she replied, studying the binoculars in her hands. She didn't want to look out the window. Didn't want to be fooled into thinking something was out there, and what's more, didn't want something—or someone—to actually be out there.

"I know what I saw."

She looked back to find him checking a pistol. She'd had no doubt there were guns hidden throughout the Carson cabin, but it was a bit of a jolt to see him efficiently working with the weapon.

He was serious, though. This was no dramatic attempt at changing the subject. His movements were too economical. His jaw was too tight. In his eyes that fierce protector light she'd always loved.

She swallowed at the mix of fear and love and turned back to the window. Lifting the binoculars with no small amount of trepidation, she studied the small part of the tree line she could make out through the natural gap in the curtain.

"I don't—" But then she did. First it was just a flash, the sun glinting off something metal. Then she could make out the faint movements of something that blended into the trees but was clearly human.

Human. Her breath caught in her throat, and for a full second or two, she was completely frozen in fear, watching the movement of someone.

"See him?"

Jen had to force herself to swallow, and then embarrassingly had to clear her throat in order to speak. "Yes," she managed, but it was little more than a croak. Fear was paralyzing her and it was demoralizing, but she couldn't seem to control it. "What do we do?"

"You stay put. I go out there and shoot him."

"You can't..." She trailed off. If this man was here to harm them, shouldn't Ty shoot him? She watched the figure, then the glint of light. What was the sun reflecting off?

"I'm not going to kill him. I want to know why the hell he's trying to torture you and me. But I'm not going to give him a chance to hurt you either. Stay put."

"I should call Laurel." But she didn't drop the binoculars. She kept thinking she could figure something out if she could only see his face.

Then she did.

And she screamed.

JEN'S SCREAM ECHOED through the cabin almost in time with a crash against the window, but the minute her scream had pierced the air, Ty had lunged.

The window glass shattered above them, pieces raining down on his back. He thought he'd protected Jen from the brunt of it, thanks to the help of the curtain that kept most of the glass contained.

"Are you okay?" he asked, panicked that

maybe something had shot through and reached her before he had.

"I'm fine," she said, her voice muffled underneath him. "What was it? A bullet?"

Ty looked at the curtain. There was a slight rip. He checked around the trajectory of the shot and frowned at what he saw.

An arrow piercing the thick area rug. Not just a flimsy Boy Scout arrow, though. This was a three-blade steel broadhead, the kind used for hunting. Which explained its impact on the window.

The window. Ty rolled off Jen, crouched and waited for someone to try to come through the window. When nothing happened, he looked down at Jen.

She was sitting now but looked dazed. "An arrow," she muttered. "That's...weird."

"A stupid, pointless stunt," Ty muttered. Oh, it was an arrow that could do some damage, but he didn't think that had been kill-shot aim. It was more scare tactics.

Ty got to his feet, done with these childish games. He flicked the safety off his pistol and strode for the door.

"Wait. Wait, Ty, there's a note." Jen crawled over to the arrow and cocked her head to read the piece of paper affixed to the back of the arrow.

Ty said something crude about what he could

do with the note, but Jen crouched down to read aloud.

"Why don't you come and find me?"

She wrinkled her nose, but Ty barely heard what she'd read aloud. Rage spread through him like a wildfire. He was nothing but heat and hate. She was bleeding. Just a little trickle from a spot on her cheek, but he'd make someone pay for that.

"I'll find him," he said, low and lethal. He reached the door, ready to jerk it open and start shooting. "I'll—"

"Ty." Jen's gentle admonition did nothing to soothe the riot of fury and worry inside him, but it did stop his forward movement. "He wants you to."

"Yeah, well, I'll give him the fight he wants." His hand was on the knob, but Jen kept talking.

"He doesn't want a fight. He could have had that back in Bent."

"He doesn't want to hurt me, then, or he could have done that, too."

"He wants to hurt you, but he's playing a game. I don't understand it, but it's a game. Come and find me—he wouldn't want you angrily going after him if he didn't have a plan to take you down."

Ty flicked the lock. "Let him try."

"Use your brain," Jen snapped with surprising force as she stalked over from where the arrow stuck out of the rug. She flicked the lock back in place and glared up at him. "He's trying to mess with you, and has been this whole time. Not only does he know we're alone up here, but he knows *us*. We don't know a darn thing about him. You don't even recognize his name. We can't underestimate him."

She'd never have any idea of how those words hurt. He knew, intellectually, she wasn't blaming him for not knowing the name, for not recognizing the man, but he felt the blame anyway.

Who had he let down? Who had he hurt? How had he lured Braxton Lynn to Bent, Wyoming, and Jen Delaney?

"You can't leave me here without my phone. I need to call Laurel," she said, sounding calm and efficient. "And you need to do something about the window. Maybe duct-tape the curtains to the wall? I know it doesn't keep him out, but it seals us in better."

"That could have hit you," he said because he didn't understand her calm. Didn't understand how she could talk about calling the police and duct-taping curtains of all things.

He needed to eliminate the threat now, and she wanted to do housekeeping.

"I know it could have." She rubbed her palm over her heart. "Or you." Her gaze met his. He'd convinced himself that ache in his heart was nostalgia or even remorse. It was sweet memories but had no bearing on the present.

Except looking at her now, knowing she could have been—and still could be hurt by all this—there was nothing *past* about it. He still loved her, deep into his bones. The kind of love time didn't dull or erase. Something all but meant to be, stitched together in whatever ruled this crazy world.

She felt it, too, in the knowledge he could have been hurt. In the realization, if she hadn't beat him to it already, that what they'd had once upon a time lived and breathed in the here and now—no matter how little either of them wanted it.

Or could have it.

He pointed to his phone on the table. "Call Laurel. I have to go out there."

"Ty—"

"Call Laurel." Then he stalked outside, ready to fight.

HE HUMMED TO HIMSELF. The shattering crash of arrow against window had been satisfying enough to put a little levity in his step.

He didn't think he'd hit anyone—surely he'd have heard a scream of pain or someone would have run out. But the fear…there had to be fear now. He looked up as he heard something. The door opening.

So, Ty had taken the bait to come after him.

He tsked under his breath. What a foolish man Ty Carson turned out to be.

Bending down, he pulled another trap out of his backpack. Antique bear trap. All steel and menace. He'd brought them lovingly back from rusty relics to shining pieces of beauty.

He hadn't been sure how or where to use them, but he'd hauled them around just the same. Now he set the three he had hefted up the hill at three separate points around the cabin.

The police would be coming soon. Surely they'd called. Gently, reverently, he pulled the trap open and set it. He watched the ragged edges glint in the light of the sun filtering through the trees.

Like a parent caressing a baby's cheek, he drifted his finger down the sharp edge. "You'll do good work for me, won't you?"

Footsteps sounded, faint but getting closer.

He had to melt away now. Luckily he was excellent at disappearing.

And reappearing when the people who deserved pain least expected it.

Chapter Eleven

Jen hated the fact she was pacing and wringing her hands like some helpless creature. The princess in the tower again. Waiting for Ty to return or the police to show up.

What kind of coward was she?

She fisted her hands on her hips. She was *choosing* the coward's way out because she was used to fading into the background and letting everyone else handle the tough stuff. The scary stuff.

Being used to something wasn't an excuse, though. She wouldn't be stupid. Leave fighting the bad guys to the people with guns they were trained and licensed to carry. It didn't mean she couldn't do *something.*

Protection. She didn't think Ty was going to find anything stomping around out there. If he did, he'd probably get hurt. At first, she shied away from that possibility, but then she stopped herself. No. She had to face facts.

He'd gone off half-cocked after a taunt from an unstable maniac. He'd put himself in danger. Luckily, Laurel was sending deputies up. They would handle whatever mess Ty had gotten himself into.

In the meantime, she needed to handle *her* mess. She was in a cabin all by herself with an unstable maniac on the loose. The man she shouldn't love, but apparently did, was off *proving* something or other. And the police were on their way.

What would they all need?

Coffee for the police. Possibly first aid for Ty. And then, she needed to protect herself.

No. Reverse all that. For once she would put herself first. Find a weapon, or ten. Then the coffee. And the dope gallivanting around the woods with a pistol could fend for himself. She'd do the first aid last.

Or so she told herself. In the end, love won out. It irritated her, but she couldn't have lived with herself if he'd staggered in bleeding like she'd imagined too many times to count already and she didn't have *something*.

Maybe it wasn't so wrong, she decided, placing the first aid kit on the table before going on a gun hunt. Maybe it wasn't about always putting others first or always putting yourself first.

Not always about asking for what you wanted, but choosing the when and knowing the why.

Maybe, it was all about *balance.*

Everything with Ty was complicated, but the feeling she had for him was simple. She pawed through a closet, turning that over in her head. Maybe in the midst of this...weirdness, she would focus on the simple.

As if on cue, she found a hunting rifle in the back corner of the closet. The chamber was empty, but she'd seen some boxes of ammunition in the tiny cabinet above the refrigerator when she'd been looking for a first aid kit.

She was no fan of guns, but her father had forced her to go hunting when she'd been a kid. All Delaneys needed to know how to hunt.

She'd hated every second of it, which had made her just another anomaly in the great Delaney clan. The rest of them might not love it, but they were good with guns, good with hunting. Jen had never had the patience or the aptitude.

She sighed heavily, grabbing the box of ammunition. Who knew being vaguely threatened by a stranger would have her rehashing so many of her childhood emotional issues?

Still, it allowed her to load the gun efficiently so she'd gotten something out of it.

She felt safer with the gun in her hand, felt

calmer with the first aid kit within reach. But she was still just *waiting.*

Before she could decide what to do about that, something at the door clicked and the door opened. She knew it would be Ty since he obviously had the key, but still she lifted the rifle.

You never knew, after all.

He stepped inside, closing and locking the door behind him before he glanced at her in the kitchen. When she didn't lower the gun, he quirked an eyebrow.

"Gonna shoot me, darling?"

Since she didn't care for his blasé tone, she used one of her own. "Considering it."

"Well, I came back unscathed, so apparently your theory about that note trying to draw me out was incorrect."

"That's what you think," Jen muttered, finally lowering the rifle. Mostly because she heard the distinct sound of a car engine, which she figured had to be the police.

Ty lifted the curtain and looked out the broken glass. He nodded. "Police. You stay here."

"Because?"

"Because."

"No. Let them come to the door. Where we'll all discuss what happened together. Rather than you taking over."

"I wasn't—"

"You were going to go out there and tell them what's what—from your perspective, and that wouldn't be a problem, except I'm the one who actually saw him shoot the arrow. You searched the woods and all, but *I* saw the whole thing happen. They'll come to the door and we'll talk to them together."

She could tell she'd surprised him. He wasn't used to her giving orders. Well, everyone was going to start getting used to it.

A knock sounded and Ty considered it. "Well, I guess you got your way."

"It's not *my* way, Ty. It's the right way." She reached past him and opened the door. She was a little disappointed Hart wasn't the deputy on the other side of the door, but he was currently working nights so it made sense. "Come in, Deputy." She gestured him inside.

"Ms. Delaney."

"I've left the arrow where it landed, and I'm sure you can see where it made impact with the window." She could feel Ty watch her as she took the deputy through the sequence of events. Still, he didn't interrupt. He didn't try to take over. He simply watched while Jen answered questions and the deputy wrote notes down in his little notebook.

"And you saw all of this, Mr. Carson?"

Ty shook his head. "No. Once I handed the binoculars over to Jen I went to get my pistol."

"The one you're wearing now?"

"Yes." He flashed the man his cocky Carson grin. "Not going to ask me if it's registered, are you?"

The deputy only grunted. Clearly he'd had enough run-ins with Carsons not to press the issue. "So you're getting the pistol—then what?"

Ty walked him through heading for the door, jumping on Jen when he heard the crash. Then her reading the letter aloud and his heading outside.

"And once you were outside, you searched for the man?"

"No. Not searched. I didn't go into the woods or look for tracks, I went to the stables."

Jen frowned. News to her. He'd let her think he was going after whoever had shot the arrow, to hurt him. But he'd gone to the stables?

"There's a hayloft up there," Ty continued. "It's rickety, but if you know where to step you can get up and get a decent view of the surrounding area. I'll admit, I'd planned to go after him, but the stables caught my eye first. I knew I'd be able to see him if he was anywhere close. But I looked all around and I didn't see anyone. There could be tracks, but I didn't want to risk it alone."

Also news to her. The jerk. She'd been worried for no reason. Maybe she should have given him more credit, but he'd been so angry when he'd huffed off. Was she really supposed to just *expect* him to make smart decisions?

Maybe the answer was yes, but she wasn't about to admit her mistake to him.

"We'll search the woods and see what we can find."

"He isn't there," Ty said flatly.

"No, but he might have left a clue behind. You let us investigate Mr. Carson and we'll—"

Ty said something crude and Jen sighed, stepping forward to smile at the deputy. "Excuse him. He's so grumpy when he hasn't had his nap. Like a toddler." She smiled at the officer, enjoying Ty's disgusted grunt. "Would you like some coffee?"

"No, ma'am, thank you. I'll join Burns out there and we'll see what we can find. If I have any more questions I'll be in touch, and we'll let you know if we find anything. And everything we find gets turned over to your sister and Deputy Hart."

"Why Hart?" Ty demanded.

The deputy eyed Ty with some disdain. "Hart is taking over as detective now that Laurel's on desk duty. He'll handle all investigations with her until she's on maternity leave, then on his own."

Ty grunted irritably. "I'll search with you."

The deputy shook his head and Jen thought Ty would bite it off if he could. So, she moved easily between law and wannabe outlaw and started ushering the police officer to the door.

"Don't worry, I'll keep him occupied while you do your *jobs*." She gave Ty a pointed look at the word, but he only stared back at her, clearly furious. But he let the deputy exit the cabin while he stayed put.

He narrowed his eyes at her once the door was shut.

"What?" she demanded loftily.

"So, you finally decided to use it."

"Use what?"

"That backbone you've been trying to ignore for almost thirty years."

HE EXPECTED HER to be pissed. That was the point after all. Undermine all this annoying confidence and take charge thing she had going on, and make her angry.

But she didn't so much as flinch. She considered.

It was beautiful to watch. This was the woman he'd always known she could be. More like her sister, but still herself. Because she'd only ever needed to stop trying to *please* everyone, including him.

She wasn't trying to please him like she had when they'd been together, and it gave him a perverse thrill. It was always the Jen he'd wanted, because he didn't deserve the girl who'd bent over backward to give everything to him. He'd never deserve her.

"I suppose that is what I decided while you let me believe you were off chasing down a madman, not looking for him from a safe vantage point."

"If I'd seen him, I'd have gone after him."

"But you didn't search the woods. You looked for him from a safe vantage point and then you came back."

Why her repetition of his very intelligent choices irritated him, he didn't know. So he shrugged. "Your point?"

"My point is you want me to believe you're this one thing—you've always wanted me to believe certain things about you, but they're very rarely true." She frowned a little, as if thinking that over. "Even leaving without a goodbye. You came home ten years later, let me believe you were just a careless jerk—even though I'd known you weren't, but the truth was you'd done it to protect me."

"Like you said earlier. I still could have said

goodbye." But he couldn't have. Not and actually done it. He hadn't been strong enough then to tell her he was leaving, to be callous and nasty and cut all ties. So, he'd taken the coward's way out.

He'd like to believe as an adult, he would have made different choices, but sometimes, when he looked into her eyes, he figured he'd always take the coward's way out when it came to hurting her.

He wanted to cross to her. Hold her. Tell her all the ways he hadn't been able to face her. Beg her to forgive him.

It unmanned him, all that swirling emotion inside. Worse, the hideous thought she might be able to see it.

"We should—" Jen was cut off by a knock on the door, thank God. "Maybe they found something," she muttered. Ty was closer, so he answered it. But it wasn't one of the deputies. It was Zach Simmons.

Ty had found out about Zach's existence only a few months ago when his aunt, who'd run away long before he'd been born, had come back to town. Zach was technically Ty's cousin, but he hadn't quite warmed to the man. Zach might be a Carson by blood, but he'd been FBI and his dad had been ATF and everything about him screamed *Delaney* to Ty—even if there weren't any Delaney ties.

So he flat out didn't trust the man. "Zach," he greeted coolly.

"Ty. Jen. Laurel called me. Sounded like you two need some security, so I hitched a ride up with a deputy," Zach said, his eyes taking in his surroundings, reminding Ty of a soldier. He wore a big black backpack and was carrying a weapon openly on his hip, and he had eyes that reminded Ty way too much of the father he'd hated. Eyes he saw in the mirror.

"We don't need security." The only reason Ty didn't slam the door in his face was the whole blood-tie thing. It wasn't Zach's fault he had the old bastard's eyes. And he'd been nothing but pleasant enough since he'd moved to Bent to work with Cam Delaney at his new security business.

But Ty didn't trust him.

"I'm pretty sure security is exactly what you need. You might not want it, but you need it," Zach returned evenly. "Laurel insisted. More, my sister insisted. You try saying no to Hilly."

It was that evenness Ty couldn't quite work out. There was a blankness to Zach, a way he kept all personality locked under a very bland shell. But he was a Carson. Even if he'd grown up away from Bent with an ATF agent father, there was Carson blood in there. A man *had* to feel it.

"Ignore him," Jen interrupted, smiling at Zach in a way that had Ty grinding his teeth together. She even took his arm and pulled him into the living room. "There's plenty of room, and I think an extra set of eyes is a good idea."

"Laurel thought so, too. She wants me to move you—"

"No," Ty said, trying for some of Zach's evenness. It came out like a barked order. "We stay where I know the turf."

Zach looked at Jen as if he was expecting her to argue. That was what Ty didn't trust about Zach. He didn't know when to stick with his own.

"I think Ty's right," Jen said, surprising him. "Clearly this man is going to track us wherever we go, and we can hardly be on the run forever. It's best to stay in a familiar place, and protect ourselves." She smiled winsomely at Zach. "Especially with a security expert around."

"I want to set up some cameras then. Nothing invasive. Just your typical security measures for dangerous lunatics lurking in the woods." He pulled the pack off his back and gave it a little pat.

"How much is that going to cost me?" Ty demanded.

Zach arched an eyebrow at him. "I suppose

I'd have to give you a family discount. It'll be borrowed equipment—we can take it all down once this is over. Consider the labor my charitable donation to a good cause."

Ty wanted to tell him they didn't need the security again, but that was knee-jerk and stupid. The more footage they had of this Braxton Lynn, the better chance they had of figuring out why he was after Ty.

"I know Laurel's investigating," Zach continued. "And I respect your sister and her work ethic. She'll work on this till she's keeling over, but she's going to investigate like a detective."

"Is there another way?" Jen asked.

"Sure. There's the FBI way, which I'm rather familiar with. There's also the bend-the-rules-so-we-can-get-our-man way. I'm a bit fond of that one." He pulled a laptop out of his backpack and placed it on the table. "Now that I'm not FBI, I'm not beholden to their rules, and I know a lot of ways to get around the bureaucratic red tape."

Ty considered the computer, then the man. He grinned. "Now you're sounding like a Carson. Let's cut some red tape, cousin."

HE GAVE IT a full twenty-four hours before he returned to the cabin. He could tell the cops had sniffed around some, but none had come close to his traps.

He was mildly disappointed, he could admit. It was for the best for his plan that no one had stumbled into one, but finding a bloody corpse or someone whose life was spilling out painfully would have lifted his spirits just a tad.

He looked up from the trap he lovingly caressed. He couldn't see the cabin from here, but he knew where it was.

Jen was probably letting Ty touch her in there. No, no. She was too pure for that. Jen Delaney seemed so kind, so good. No, Ty was probably forcing himself upon her. She was a victim, and it was his duty to save her.

He rubbed at the headache that began to drum. No, that was all wrong. Ty needed to pay, but he could do that only through Jen. Ty had irreparably damaged Oscar.

Ty had broken his brother when they'd been in the army. It was the only explanation, and once he'd gotten through to Oscar, Oscar had agreed it was all Ty's fault. Other people were always to blame for Oscar's shortcomings, but he'd come up with a way to fix that. To get Oscar on his side again.

He would break Ty's woman, for Oscar. It was only fair. Sometimes innocents were hurt because bad men roamed the world. Bad men needed to be hurt. They needed to suffer.

Once Ty did, his own suffering would go away.

He looked down at his shaking hands. He was getting too far out of control. The plan was hazy and he wasn't focused on the goal. The goal.

It was all this waiting. All this planning. Vengeance needed to wait and be planned, but a hero acted. A hero did what he came here to do.

He would be Oscar's hero. *Now.*

Chapter Twelve

The next morning, Jen was happy to make breakfast for the two men she was temporarily sharing a cabin with. She might have discovered her backbone yesterday, or trusted it enough to use it, but she'd long ago decided she'd rather make the meals her way than be waited on.

Zach had spent most of yesterday tapping away on his computer conferring with Ty in low tones about what little they knew about Braxton Lynn, going over the layout of the cabin and where they could feasibly install cameras.

They had a plan for the cameras now, but Zach hadn't been able to find much about the man.

Frustrated, they'd called it a night, and now today was a fresh day. Zach was going to install his surveillance equipment, then try his hand at some hacking.

Jen had felt superfluous. At best. Last night and now, but she didn't know how to set up cameras or hack into government records, or anything about Braxton or Ty's military past, so she'd had to accept it. This wasn't her time.

But she'd listened, and she'd come up with her own conclusions. She'd always been good at observing people and reading them. If you were going to contort yourself to be what someone else wanted, or try, you had to understand them on some level.

The man after Ty didn't want something as simple as just to hurt him. He wanted to *torture* Ty, terrorize him, using whatever means—family or past lovers—to do it. The question was, why didn't he focus on Ty's family, the most important thing to him?

There was the most obvious reason, one that made Jen's gut burn with shame. She was the easy target. Carsons were rough and tough and harder to threaten. She was weak and easy pickings.

Well, no thank you.

She let Ty and Zach settle into breakfast as she sipped her coffee and watched them eat and discuss. Like she wasn't even there.

No thank you to that, too.

"You're going about this the wrong way," she announced casually, so irritated with them and herself that it didn't even bother her when they both gave her the same patently Carson questioning look. Eyebrow raised, mouth quirked, with just enough disbelief in their gaze to make a person feel stupid.

She refused.

"You're thinking about this like he's after *me*, when we know he's trying to hurt Ty."

"No. He's trying to hurt *you* because of me."

She rolled her eyes. "Let's try to step outside of macho egomaniac land for one second. Yes, he wants to hurt you. But how? Emotionally, not physically."

"So?"

"So? Everything you're planning is physical. And factual. He's not interested in either thing. He doesn't want to physically hurt you. He wants to terrorize you via someone you care about. Even when you're trying to figure out his connection to you, it's only so you know his identity, so you can identify and isolate his threat. But what you need to be doing is trying to understand him."

"How can we understand him if we don't know who he is?" Zach asked reasonably.

"But we do know. We know his name. We know his foster sister reported him missing, but no one's really looking for him. So, what does that tell you?"

"Not a whole lot."

Ty shook his head. "She's right," he said, with no small amount of irritation. "He's alone in the world. No one really cares about him. Which means you can make the reasonable connection that whoever he's looking to avenge *did* care about him, or he thought they did."

"Exactly. And if he's blaming Ty, out to terrorize Ty, he blames Ty for losing this mystery person. Maybe they died, or maybe they left him. Maybe there's something else, but he wants Ty to hurt the way *he* hurts. The key isn't Braxton or me, it's the link."

Both men stared at her, with no small amount of doubt in their expressions. And they were so quiet and military still, Jen fidgeted with her coffee mug. She didn't let herself blurt out the apologies or *at least that's what I think* that filled her brain.

She knew, *knew*, whether they agreed or not, her theory had more merit than the way they were currently going about things.

"I can't discount it," Zach returned, still frowning as if considering and finding her lacking.

No, not *her*. Her theory. She needed to be better about acknowledging that difference.

"But I can't wrap my head around it either.

It doesn't make sense why anyone would get it all so mixed up in their head."

"You're trying to reason it out," Ty interrupted. "I think what Jen's saying is it's not the kind of reason that's going to make sense to, well, reasonable people."

"Exactly," Jen said, emboldened by Ty's understanding. "You can't think about facts and reason, you have to think about the emotion. Revenge is led by emotion."

"You have to consider both," Zach countered. "You've got a good point. His motivation isn't one we're necessarily going to understand because clearly he's not well. But if we know who *he* is, identity-wise, we have a better idea of how to deal with his emotion *and* a better shot at finding the missing link. Facts and emotion need a balance."

Jen considered that. "I suppose you're right. Fact informs the emotion side of things, even if it's not a straight line."

Zach grinned at her. "Can you say that again? 'I suppose you're right.' I've never heard any Carson or Delaney or Simmons for that matter say anything remotely admitting I'm right. I think you're the most reasonable person in the whole dang bunch."

Jen flushed with pleasure.

"Maybe you'd like me to leave you two alone," Ty grumbled.

Jen rolled her eyes at him and got to her feet, clearing the breakfast dishes, but Zach was taking them out of her hand before she could make it to the sink.

"I should do that. You made breakfast. I'll clean up."

It was her first instinct to argue, to insist she did the work she knew she could do. But she wasn't here because she could cook or clean. She wasn't here to take care of everyone while they did the important work.

No.

She was here because she'd been put in danger. Maybe Zach and Ty were here to protect her, but that didn't mean she had to take care of everything.

Wow. It was a lightning bolt of a thought. That she didn't have to be the one to clean up all the messes to earn her place here. That she didn't have to bend over backward to do whatever was asked of her simply because everyone else was more qualified to handle the threat against them.

Because the threat was against her, too.

So, she beamed at Zach and let him take the dishes. "Thank you. I'm going to go call Hilly and see how the store is faring." And she was going to spend some time thinking about how when this was all over, she was going to make sure her life changed.

"SURE IS A pretty little thing. Good cook, too."

Ty looked at where Zach was cheerfully washing the breakfast dishes. He was so shocked by the casual commentary all he could seem to manage was, "Excuse me?"

Zach shrugged. "Best breakfast I've had in a while."

When Ty only stared, Zach kept yammering on.

"Certainly the prettiest scenery I've had for breakfast in a *long* while. Maybe ever. Something about sweet—"

"That'll be enough," Ty interrupted, pushing away from the table.

"What? Am I breaking some Carson code? Not supposed to admit a Delaney is pretty as a picture and nice to have around? Figured that nonsense was on the way out with the way everyone's pairing off. Carsons and Delaneys seem destined to end up saying 'I do' in this particular point in history." Zach stopped drying a plate, an overly thoughtful expression on his face. "She's a Delaney. Technically I'm a Carson. I suppose—"

"I said, that'll be enough."

Zach surprised him by laughing and turned back to finishing the dishes. "You've got it *bad*."

Ty blinked. "I don't—"

"I don't see much point in denying everything. Everyone seems to know you two had something way back when, and it doesn't take my former FBI training to figure out it's still simmering under the surface." He shrugged negligently as he put away the last plate. "Why don't you do something about it instead of stomping around snarling like a lion with a thorn in its paw?"

It was horrifying to be seen through so easily by someone he barely knew, so he went for derision. "Yeah, let's just forget the unstable maniac shooting arrows at us."

"Haven't seen an arrow yet today. Even unstable maniacs have to rest, and the fact of the matter is, your brain's going to be a lot clearer if you do something other than brood."

"I don't brood."

"You do an excellent imitation of it, then."

"What business is that of yours?" Ty demanded sharply.

Zach raised an eyebrow with enough condescension in his expression to remind Ty irritably of Grady.

"Absolutely none," Zach replied, pleasantly enough. He wiped his hands on a dish towel and nodded toward the door. "I'm going to set up the cameras like we talked about."

How that made Ty feel guilty was beyond him. He had nothing to feel guilty about. Zach might technically be his cousin, but it wasn't like they'd grown up together. He hadn't even known Zach existed until a couple of months ago. Why would he take advice or ribbing from a virtual stranger?

But as Zach stepped outside, his pack with all its surveillance equipment and computer nonsense on his back, Ty felt *awash* in familial guilt—the kind he hadn't entertained for a very long time. He shook his head and walked to the room he'd given over to Zach last night to just have a second of privacy to…something.

But he had to pass by the open door to the room Jen was in, where she was happily making the bed—whistling. Her cheerfulness scraped across every last raw nerve.

He scowled at her back. "Hart. Zach. You really go for the law-and-order type."

She straightened, leveling him with a look he didn't recognize. "I suppose it's better than the idiot, pea-brained jealous-for-no-reason type." She smiled at him, a surprisingly vicious edge to it.

There had to be something a little screwy in him that even as irritation simmered in his gut, he liked the idea of Jen getting a little vicious. "I am not jealous." Which he knew, very well, was the thing someone said when that was exactly the ugly thing worming around in the person's gut.

Zach calling her pretty, even if it was just to mess with him—it made him feral. It made him want to stake some claim he had no business claiming.

"No, not jealous," Jen said with a dismissive edge. "You just have to be snotty anytime another man even acknowledges I exist. Even though *you* don't acknowledge I exist half the time. Wouldn't, if I wasn't being threatened because of something *you* did."

"Is that some kind of complaint? Pretty sure you've been avoiding me as skillfully as I've been avoiding you since I've been home."

"So you admit it, then?"

"Admit what?"

"That you've avoided me."

He couldn't figure her out, or why there was now a headache drumming at his temples and all he really wanted to do was scoop her up and make good use of that freshly made bed. "Why's that an admission? We were both doing it."

She stepped closer, poked him in the chest. "Yeah, we both were. We both were. I thought it was because you didn't care, but what an idiot I was. It was because you felt the same way I did."

He crossed his arms over his chest, trying to look disdainful instead of whatever uncomfortable thing fluttered in his chest, squeezing his lungs. "And what way's that?"

"Hurt. You were hurting just as I was." She searched his face, so he did everything he could to keep it impassable.

Hurt had always been the enemy. You showed you were hurt, you got knocked around a little extra hard. Literal or metaphorical in his experience with life.

But here she was, calling it what it was, saying they'd both been walking around with it deep inside them. She was cracking away at something inside him, letting something loose he wouldn't name. Couldn't.

"You know what? I wish I *did* go for the 'law and order' type. I wish Hart or Zach were exactly what I wanted out of life. They're both polite. Kind. Good men who want to do the right thing and aren't afraid to admit it. In other words, the antithesis of *you*. But I…" She took a deep breath and squared her shoulders. She looked like she was getting ready to do battle, and he was…

Scared. That thing she was pulling out of him, that feeling a strong, immovable Carson was never supposed to feel over some *woman*. It stole over him, shamed him deeply that he was bone-deep scared of what this slip of a woman was going to say to him.

He allowed himself to recognize the fear, acknowledge it. Even accepted the fact it was worse than any fear he'd had in the army, because death hadn't seemed so bad. At least it would have been a noble one.

There was nothing noble or impressive about being scared of the woman who held your heart. No. So he would not be a coward no matter how he felt like one. He squared, too, and prepared for the blow.

"I love you," she said, and she certainly knew every one of those words was an unerring bullet against his heart. "Yeah, I love you, you big, overbearing moron. I have always loved you and I always will. And I want to punch you. And I'm still mad at the way you left, but understanding it means I can forgive, and I *do*."

"Don't." He choked it out, rough and telling. But the emotion that clogged his throat, that made his heart feel too big and beating in his chest, was winning against all control. It was this, right here, that had been his reason for leaving her without saying goodbye.

He wouldn't have ever been able to look at her and hide all those things he felt. He wasn't strong enough to hurt her, even for her own good. Not to her face anyway. He'd never be strong enough for that.

"It'd be awful for you, wouldn't it?" she asked, tears swimming and making her eyes look luminous. "If I didn't hold a grudge. If I just forgave you. Because then you'd have to forgive yourself, and that's the one thing you've never been any good at."

"I said stop."

"No, no. I'm done stopping for someone else's comfort." She stepped so close he could smell her, that light feminine scent that always seemed to float around her. He could feel the warmth of her—not just generic body warmth, but that piece of her soul that had drawn him long before he'd been willing to admit souls even existed.

Was he willing to admit that now? He didn't know.

When she touched him, her palm to his heart, he winced. The look she shot him was triumphant. Determined. And so damn strong he thought she might bring him to his knees.

"I love you," she said, her eyes never leaving his. "I *want* you."

He tried to move away, but so much of him was suddenly made out of lead and her hand fisted in his shirt, keeping him right where he was. In this nightmare where she said things he wanted and shouldn't have.

Couldn't. The word is couldn't.

"And what scares you, what horrifies you, is that you love and want me, too," she continued, hammering every last nail in the coffin that was his self-control. His belief that he could control his life, his emotions, his choices.

"But you know you'd have to forgive yourself for that love. You'd have to look back at seventeen-year-old Ty and think he actually did the best he could in the situation he was given. You'd have to look back at little ten-year-old Ty and forgive him for letting his dad knock him and his brother around, forgive yourself for not killing him when he started knocking Vanessa around, too. There's so much you'd have to stop blaming yourself for to admit you love me, that we deserve each other—then and now."

If there were words to be salvaged out of this nightmare, he didn't have them. She must have taken them all, because they kept pouring out of her.

"I should have said all that to you when you got back into town, because I knew it then even when I didn't know why you left. I've always known it. But I was too afraid to tell you what I knew, what I saw. I wanted to make you comfortable instead of making us...well, what would have endured. But I was seventeen, too. Young and scarred in my own ways, because we *always* are, Ty. All of us. Scarred and scared and uncertain. We're all doing the best we can with what we have."

He closed his eyes, but her other hand came to his cheek. He didn't want to believe her. She had to hate him for what he'd done—because he hated himself for the way he'd left. For the way he'd come back. He couldn't blame the latter on a young man with few choices. He'd been an adult, and he'd continued to act like she didn't matter.

Still, she touched him like forgiveness wasn't just possible. It was done. A given. Something she wouldn't take back.

"Open your eyes, Ty."

He did, because he seemed to have no power here. She was in control. She gave the orders, and he obeyed, excellent soldier that he was.

But it was more than that. No matter how much he didn't want to believe he could have her, no matter how much he knew he didn't deserve her, his heart still wanted.

"I love you," she said, and it didn't hurt so much the second time. "And you love me. That's where we'll start."

So much of his scars and his past fought to win, to deny. But she was touching him, staring at him. Drowning in her eyes, he lost the battle with himself.

"No. This is where we start," he replied, covering her mouth with his.

THEY DIDN'T KNOW they were being watched.

Chapter Thirteen

It was home. Ty's kiss had always been exactly where Jen belonged, and somehow she had made it happen again.

So she threw herself into it, into him, wrapping herself around him with what she might have called desperation just days ago.

But she wasn't desperate. No. She was determined. She had finally figured out what she wanted, what she was willing to fight for, and it didn't matter if they were hiding out from danger or if they went home to Bent right now.

He was hers.

His hands streaked over her, rough and possessive. She returned the favor. He scraped his teeth across her bottom lip, so she dug her fingernails into his shoulders. Her knees buckled, but he held her up hard against his chest.

And then it all softened, as if all the tension simply leaked out of him. As if he was giving in to more than just the driving attraction that had always been between them. His mouth softened, his hands gentled. He held her as if she was spun glass and kissed her as if she were the center of his universe.

He was giving in to love.

She'd chosen it years ago, but she hadn't been mature enough to understand that. She'd called it fate or divine intervention, but it had been her. Her wanting him, and his wanting her. She'd been afraid of the consequences, but that had only made it more exciting.

Ten years later the excitement wasn't in thwarting her family's expectation, it was in the choice. In the knowledge of all that time, in the changes she'd made inside herself and the changes she hadn't made, he was still where she belonged.

The dull ring of a phone pierced the fog in her brain, but with her body humming and desperate for more of Ty, she didn't really acknowledge it. It couldn't be all that important, could it? Not as important as this.

Except, of course, it might be. Because they were not just realizing and deciding all these big, life-changing things in the midst of a normal day.

She managed to move her mouth away from his, though she kept her arms tight around him, and couldn't resist pressing a kiss to his jaw. "Phone."

"Nah." His hands slid up under her shirt, over the cotton of her bra. Hot and rough, he dragged his fingertips across the peaks of her nipples.

"It could, uh..." What was she talking about? It was hard to remember with need curling low in her stomach. But the phone kept jangling and somewhere in the fog of desperate lust she understood... "It could be important."

"Why would it—" He managed to lift his head, his expression as dazed as she felt. But he narrowed his eyes. "I guess it could be." But the sound died and they looked at each other, still holding on, still not close enough.

He lowered his mouth. "We'll just forget—"

But it immediately started ringing again and they both sighed. Ty let her go, and she had to sink onto the bed. Her legs simply wouldn't hold her.

He pulled the phone out of his pocket, frowned at the screen, then handed it to her. "Your sister. Why don't you answer it."

Jen cocked her head at the screen as she swiped to answer. "We can talk about why my sister is in your phone as Deputy PITA later." She lifted the receiver to her ear and answered, trying to sound breezy and light.

She was pretty sure she sounded deranged.

"Is everything okay?" Laurel asked without preamble, worry enhancing the demand in her tone. "Are you safe?"

"Safe? Of course. Everything is great. Everything is… Yes."

There was a long, contemplative silence over the phone and Jen had to squeeze her eyes shut and try to get a hold of herself.

But what she really wanted was a hold of Ty and to banish this ache that felt as though it had been growing inside her for a decade.

"You were commandeered to the Carson cabin by your ex—who left you without explanation ten years ago. You're in danger because someone who wants to hurt him thinks hurting you will do the trick. But you're great?"

Though Jen had gotten her breathing somewhat closer to being in control, she couldn't look at Ty or she'd never be able to have a coherent conversation. So, she stared at her lap and focused on the fact Laurel was calling them.

"I'm just making the best out of a bad situation," she offered brightly.

"Is that best in Ty Carson's pants?"

"Laurel!" Jen managed through strangled laughter. It was a little too apt.

"Well, you're panting like you're running away from a bad guy or…"

"Did you call for a reason?" Jen asked primly,

wondering just how red her cheeks were and just what Ty would read into her embarrassment over her sister's seeing right through her even over the phone.

"Yes. Actually. I want to talk to both of you on Speaker, and Zach if he's there. I think I'm hoping he's not there or things would be weird."

"He's out putting up some of his surveillance equipment," Jen grumbled.

"Okay, that's fine. You can fill him in. Put me on Speaker. Unless Ty's naked. I don't want to talk to Ty on Speaker if he's naked."

"He's not..." Fumbling with his phone, Jen managed to switch on Speaker. She avoided Ty's steady gaze even though she felt it boring into her. She cleared her throat. "Laurel has some news."

"The DNA on your notes matches Braxton Lynn," Laurel announced. "And here's where things get interesting. We looked into the name you gave us, Ty. Oscar Villanueva of Minnow, Arizona. Turns out he and Braxton Lynn lived in the same group home for four years."

"He's connected to Oscar," Ty said dully.

Jen reached out and gave his hand a squeeze. Though she didn't know why it should hit him hard, she could tell from that voice devoid of all emotion it *did* hit him.

"Yes. I'm still working on information, but

Braxton's behavior became erratic after Oscar left for the army. Bounced around different foster situations, and I wouldn't be surprised if he had some criminal issues, but I don't have any access to juvenile records. Which is why I want you to pass that along to Zach."

"You're telling me you, Ms. Law and Order, know full well Zach is hacking into closed files?" Ty asked incredulously.

"Don't sound so surprised. I *am* married to Grady. Something had to rub off. Besides, I'm not asking him to. I just know he can and probably is. So, give him the name and if he finds anything, I want to know. My men searched the woods. A few footprints, but nothing concrete enough to figure out where he disappeared to, so I want you two to stay put for the time being. Now that we're sure that it's him, we should be able to round him up soon enough."

"Where's Oscar?" Ty asked.

There was no answer, only the slight buzz of a phone connection. Jen looked up, her heart twisting at that blank expression on his face.

"Laurel." Ty's voice was quiet and calm, but Jen could see the tension in him underneath that stoic mask.

"It seems as if Oscar's been in a lot of trouble since he got out of the army," Laurel said gently, and vaguely Jen noted. "Since he was *kicked* out of the army I should say, but you knew that, didn't you?"

"Yeah, I knew."

"Is it possible that has something to do with Braxton's fixation on you? Oscar, his foster brother, was booted out, and you went into the rangers?"

Jen watched Ty rake his hands through his hair. And there it was—all that guilt he heaped upon himself. "Yeah. Not possible. Probable. I reported Oscar's dependence on drugs and alcohol to our superiors. It directly resulted in Oscar's discharge."

"You didn't think to tell me that a little sooner?" Laurel demanded.

"No, I didn't. I didn't think they could be connected. Or maybe I didn't want them to be. I'll apologize for that, but it doesn't change anything."

"We should focus on Braxton," Jen said. She tried to reach for Ty's hand again, but he moved away from her. Out of reach. "Obviously he blames Ty for something, but Oscar having some trouble with the law—"

"He's in prison."

Jen closed her eyes. She didn't know the man, and yet her heart ached for what this would all do to Ty.

"I have to go," Laurel said, sounding understandably tired. No doubt she was putting in too many hours on top of pregnancy. "Fill Zach in. Keep yourselves safe. Got it?"

"Yeah. Thanks, Laurel," Jen managed. "Keep us updated."

"I will. Stay safe."

The call ended and Jen looked at Ty. He had his back to her, so rigid. Everything about him radiated *do not touch* energy. Her first instinct was to give him space, even as her heart ached to touch him. To soothe.

Her heart had been leading her today, not her instincts. So, she'd be brave enough to follow her heart again. She crossed the room to him, wrapped her arms around him from behind and leaned her cheek against his back.

TY DIDN'T WANT her comfort. That was what he told himself. He didn't want soft arms or sweet words. It was better, so much better, when you learned to do without. Because you could forget. You could convince yourself you didn't need it.

God, he needed her. Even something as simple as this hug kept that heavy blackness of guilt from consuming him completely.

But it slithered along the edges. The connection to Oscar made so much sense. He'd thought about Oscar on and off over the years. Ty had always felt bad for the way things had shaken out, but he'd known Oscar was a liability to everyone around him. He thought getting him booted home might be some kind of a favor.

Instead it had been a life sentence. Prison.

How could it not be his fault? His action had directly led to Oscar's discharge. Maybe bad things would have happened to Oscar either way, but it was hard to hold on to that when he could only think of all the ways he could have done it differently.

"Don't," Jen murmured.

He stiffened. "Don't what?" he asked, knowing exactly what she'd say.

She moved to his front and reached up to brush her fingers over his close-cropped hair. "You know what. Don't blame yourself for someone else's actions. We're too old for that now."

He could have shrugged her off. He could have ignored it all and focused on the task at hand: Braxton Lynn and his fixation on Jen. Instead, faced with her sympathetic brown eyes and her kiss and "I love yous" drifting through his mind, only the truth could spill out.

"I ratted him out, Jen. Now he's in prison. How am I not supposed to draw some conclusions on my guilt?"

"You informed your superiors of a problem

because he was a potential threat—not just to others, but to himself."

"How did you…" But he realized she didn't *know* it. She just figured it out. She was always good at that—working out why people felt the way they did, thought the way they did, acted the way they did.

"So, say it."

He didn't want to. Partially because he couldn't believe it and partially because of that same emotion that had jolted him earlier. Fear. But again, he wouldn't let fear win. "It wasn't my fault," he intoned, even though it was a lie.

"Now, work on believing it." She smiled and then lifted on her toes to brush her mouth against his.

She kissed him like she believed he was worthy of it or her. She always had, and he'd figured it for a lack in judgment. A lack he took advantage of because he couldn't help himself.

But her judgment was just fine, and she understood him all too well. Still she loved him. Over years and distance, she loved him and was willing to forgive him. Forgive *him*.

"What are we going to do about this?" he asked, and he didn't have to specify which *this*. She clearly knew.

She smiled. "Embrace it."

He watched the man. He still hadn't figured out who this third wheel was, and he didn't like it.

He didn't like anything right now. Through the night he'd managed to drill a hole in the room he'd figured to be a bedroom based on one of the few windows and cheerful curtains.

All while cops had tramped around in the night, loud and stupid, he had worked. It had been so easy to stand in the shadow against the cabin and quietly and carefully drill his hole. Everyone said his old-fashioned tools were pointless. But they were quiet. They were gruesomely effective.

He'd gotten a perfect hole to insert the tiny camera. Modern technology had its place, too. He appreciated the old and the antique of a simpler, better time, but Oscar had taught him how to use the modern, too. He'd taught him to drive when no one in that house had cared about him.

Oscar had been his big brother. They didn't need blood to have a bond.

But then Oscar had left. Tempted away by the army and their lies about bravery and courage and meaning something.

He would have followed. Had planned on it. But then Oscar had gotten thrown out.

Ty's fault.

Oscar had started getting into trouble. Oscar hadn't wanted him around anymore.

Ty's fault.

All of it, all the bad before he'd finally gotten his brother back was Ty's fault.

Maybe he'd been a little grateful for Oscar's prison time, because Oscar didn't have a choice anymore. If Oscar wanted a visit from the outside, it was from him. He didn't tell Oscar that, though. Instead, he told Oscar he would make everything right. Balance the scales so they were brothers again.

Oscar had liked the idea. Liked the idea of hurting anyone who'd harmed him.

First it was the girl in Phoenix. She'd led Oscar on, and then Oscar had had no choice but to hurt her. But Oscar had landed in jail, and the girl had gotten off scot-free.

He'd fixed that, and Oscar had been very appreciative. Oscar had even called him *brother* again.

He had to close his eyes to rid them of the tears that clouded his vision. They'd been brothers again.

And once he paid back Ty for all the ways he'd hurt Oscar, they'd be a real family. For good. No matter what.

He narrowed his eyes at the man walking out of the stables. This stranger was putting up surveillance equipment.

That wouldn't do.

He knelt and pulled the pack off his back and surveyed his weapon options. He wanted to save the bear traps for Ty, though anyone who wandered across them would be fine, but he wouldn't lure this stranger to one. The arrows were for Jen. She needed some comeuppance for the way she'd let Ty touch her.

The gun would probably be too loud. He pulled the pistol out, aimed it, pretended to fire. Then chuckled to himself. He was nothing if not resourceful. Why take out the stranger now when he could get two for the price of one?

And then Jen would be his.

She would need to be punished.

He was starting to ache for that. For her screams. For her blood.

She isn't your focus. She's only a tool to get to Ty.

But if she was only a tool, that meant whatever was left over could be his. Screams, blood and all.

Chapter Fourteen

Jen managed only a few bites of her canned chili dinner. Zach had hacked into the juvenile records system, and his expression was grim as he got ready to tell them what he'd found. It made her stomach churn.

"Unfortunately, this isn't the kind of record I'd want to see knowing said person is out there haunting the woods."

"That bad?"

"It looks like it started small. He's got some vague notes in his foster files about erratic behavior, threats of violence. A few assault charges he was given some leeway on since he was so young and bounced around. Things kind of level off, then spike up again right around the time Oscar would have left for the army. Stalking, assault—mostly against women. It looks like he had mandatory counseling as he got closer to eighteen."

"Clearly it solved all his problems," Ty returned drily.

"Record-wise? It seems to have helped. He doesn't have anything as an adult. Not so much as a speeding ticket. He left the group home as soon as he could. Had trouble keeping a job, but other than that..."

"Mostly against women," Jen murmured, turning that small piece of information over in her mind. It had to be relevant, and possibly the key. "And yet, his anger is directed at Ty, but he's chosen me as a target."

"He views you as weaker. A safer target," Zach offered.

"Yes. His behavior now... He has to know he's going to get in trouble—after years of not getting into any."

"Just because there's no record of it doesn't mean he didn't do anything wrong. It just means he wasn't caught," Ty pointed out.

"It's more likely," Zach agreed. "The lengths to which he's willing to go now doesn't point to an emotionally stable soul, or a man who was rehabilitated, then snapped back."

"If his violence is typically against women, then that's our answer." It explained the lack of action. She was stuck in a cabin with a former army ranger and a former FBI agent, so that would be threatening to Braxton. If they were going to draw him out, end this, it needed to be with someone he didn't find threatening. It just made sense. But then Ty laughed.

Not a real laugh—a harsh, sarcastic sound that had her bristling. "No," he said simply, as if she'd outlined her plan out loud, as if his word was final.

"You don't know what I was going to say."

"Of course I know what you were going to say. You're a Delaney, aren't you?" He pushed out of his chair and began to pace.

She was surprised enough by the angry strides to be quiet for a few seconds. He wasn't even trying to hide his irritation. It simmered around him plain as day, with every footstep one way and every whirl to pace in the opposite direction. Which wasn't like Ty at all.

"I don't know what being a Delaney has to do with the fact that a woman won't be threatening to him, and we need to draw him out."

"Addie did the same thing, didn't she?" Ty demanded, eyes blazing. "She tried to use herself as bait. And what happened?"

Jen frowned. She hated to think back to the way Addie had been kidnapped and hurt. Terrorized really, but she'd survived. And the man who'd hurt her couldn't anymore. "This isn't the same as the *mob*, Ty. I believe you pointed that out to me just a few days ago when I reminded you that Noah bringing Addie here hadn't exactly worked out for them back then."

"You're not going to be the lure, darling, so get it out of your head."

"Oh, well, you've told me," she replied, letting the sarcasm drip from her tone without trying to soften it any. She pretended to salute him. "Yes, sir. Et cetera."

Zach cleared his throat. "Maybe I could be the tiebreaker?"

They both glared at him with such venom he cleared his throat again. "And maybe I'll leave you two to argue it out. I'll go to my room and, er, watch the surveillance tape."

Jen didn't even watch him go. She turned her glare back to Ty. He was scowling at her.

"Do you think I'm weak?" she demanded.

He didn't even flinch, or hesitate. "No."

She had to admit it soothed her irritation a little bit. Until he kept talking.

"But I think this is my fight. And you know what? Ten years in the military, yeah, I think I've got a little better handle on a psychopath who hates women than you do."

"That's doesn't mean—"

"Yes, it does. You will stay put. You will do as I say."

"Do as you…" Rage tinged her vision red.

"You think you can order me around simply because I love you? Well, think again, Mister."

"Are you really going to keep saying that?"

"Yes, I am. I love you a million times over, but you will not boss me around like I'm still seventeen and need a keeper. What we have now is an adult relationship, Ty, and we're going to treat each other like adults."

He stared at her. All that irritable energy that had been pumping off him was gone, somehow wrapped up and shoved beneath this impenetrable veneer.

Then he softened. Not so much visibly—he was still all rigid military muscle, but that fighter's light in his eyes dimmed and he stepped toward her.

"I can't stand the thought of it, Jen," he said, his voice rough as he laid his hands on her shoulders. "You getting hurt in all this."

She didn't smile, though she wanted to. It was almost as if her whole life had been building to this moment—danger mixed with love, hope mixed with fear. "Tell me why," she murmured, leaning into him. "Besides your incessant need to heap guilt upon yourself."

For a hair of a second he went stiff, and honestly it soothed her as well as the gradual softening, the way his arms came around her. It wasn't *easy* for him to love her. She'd always known that. It was the fact he'd do it anyway that had always meant the world to her. Love meant facing down all his fears and guilt, and he did so. For her.

It made the forgiveness for all that had come before easier and easier. It watered the seeds of determination until fear didn't have room to grow.

They'd come through this because they'd come so far. They'd find a way to work together to get home because now they got to go home together.

"I can't stand the thought of you getting hurt because I love you. Which you said you already knew," he grumbled.

"Doesn't hurt to hear." She sighed. "We're a team. I'm not a person you're protecting," she muttered into his chest. "It's not fair to use love against me to try to keep me safe and locked away."

He kissed her hair. "Who said I was going to be fair?"

"We have to do something. We can't stay shut up here forever. I have to get back to my store. I have to—we have to—get back to our lives. I don't want to wait around for the next note. I want to go home."

He pulled her back, though he held on to her shoulders. He looked into her eyes.

"I'll get you home. I promise you that."

"I don't need you to. I need you to work with me. For the three of us to work as a team so we can *all* go home. I want you to promise me we're in this together, not that you'll get me home."

He pulled a face, but he didn't let her go, didn't move away. So she traced her fingers along his scruffy jaw.

"I need that promise from you, Ty. As much as I need your love. Love might exist without teamwork and communication, but I think we both learned it doesn't *work* without it."

He sighed heavily, clearly struggling to agree, even though there was no way he could disagree. It was their simple truth, whether either of them liked it or not.

"I can't promise not to act instinctively to protect you. I can't promise to let you get hurt if I see a way around it, even if it hurts me. I can't promise you that."

"So, what are you going to promise me?"

"Just how demanding is new Jen going to be?"

She grinned at him, because she liked the idea. New Jen and more *demanding.* No, she'd never demanded things for herself. But now she would. Because life didn't protect the good girls who bent over backward to make other people happy, any more than it protected women who did the opposite. Life was undiscerning, and there was no cosmic reward of safety.

"Yeah, I think new Jen is demanding, but fair."

He swept his hand over the crown of her head. "New Jen's not so bad."

"Uh-huh. So, where's my promise?"

He grunted, but he held on to her shoulders, kept her gaze. "I promise that the three of us work together to get home safely. No secrets, no sacrificial plans. We're going to be smart. And we're going to work together."

Jen rose to her toes and pressed her mouth to his. "That's a fine promise."

HE WASN'T HAPPY about the promise. In fact, it sat heavy in his gut like a weight through the rest of the evening. Just like the knowledge Oscar was in prison. Just like the knowledge Jen was right.

They couldn't stand around waiting for the guy to make a move. Eventually they had to go home.

It was a surprise to him that Jen had flipped it all on its head. He wanted to go home. He wanted to live that life they'd planned, but with this new version of themselves—strong and smarter and capable of facing down the world. Facing Bent and her father and the incessant ribbing they'd surely get from their siblings and cousins.

He welcomed that.

He'd been a coward. He could admit that now, in the dark on this uncomfortable couch. Grady had been right. He ran away, not from dangerous situations, but from emotions. From love and hope and the things his childhood had taught him were traps.

But his brother, his cousins and Jen had all proved that wrong for him, and it was time to stop being ruled by his past. By the guilt of the abused.

He looked over at the door to the room Jen was in. He'd given Zach the other bedroom since the guy had all sorts of equipment. Besides, didn't he deserve to be the one on the couch since this was all his fault?

But Jen didn't blame him. Not for any of it. She loved him, forgave him and thought they could embrace a future together.

It had only taken a threat against her for him to see it, believe it might be possible. There was guilt there, too, and he knew it would be easy to stay on this uncomfortable couch and drown in it. He'd always let himself drown in it, considered his guilt so brave.

But Jen had called it childish, and as much as he wanted to tell himself—and her—that she didn't know what she was talking about, of course she did. She'd always known what she was talking about more than he did.

He rolled off the couch, surprised to find himself as shaky as he'd ever been facing down a dangerous mission.

This wasn't dangerous, but it was daunting. This wasn't life or death, but it was Jen's heart and for that he'd face life or death. He walked to the door to her room. He paused, breathing through the unfamiliar nerves.

If he went into this room, he was making promises he couldn't take back. He was accepting everything Jen had said. He was forgiving himself for a past he'd always blamed himself for.

Can you really do that?

He never thought the answer to that question would be yes, but it was. Because Jen had forgiven him, and she was the best person he knew. She had to be right in her forgiveness, so he'd believe in her, and forgiveness of self would follow.

He turned the knob, slipped into the dark room.

"Oh, Zach, is that you?" she murmured sleepily.

She was lucky he knew better. "You're a real laugh a minute."

She chuckled, so pleased with herself he couldn't help but find himself smiling in the dark. She'd always been his joy in the dark.

"What took you so long?" she demanded.

"I guess I had some things to work out." Even with no light, he knew exactly how many steps to the bed, what side she'd be sleeping on. He toed off his boots and then lowered himself onto the mattress.

She rolled into him, pulling the covers over him. No hesitation. She'd made her decision, and it wouldn't waver. He couldn't either.

He pulled her close, his decision made, no matter where it took them. "I don't take it lightly."

She snuggled in. "I know. I don't either." She pressed a kiss to his jaw. "Make love to me, Ty."

"I figured a rousing game of gin rummy would be more my speed."

"Hmm." She kissed his temple, his cheek, his neck. "Are you sure about that?" she murmured, her hand drifting under his T-shirt.

He rolled her underneath him. "On second thought."

She laughed, tugging at his shirt. "Oh, hurry. It's been too long."

Far too long, so he did exactly what she asked. He hurried. They tugged off each other's clothes with more desperation than nimble fingers. He couldn't get enough of her, worse than the kiss earlier today because she was naked underneath him. His. Always.

They came together on a sigh, and it didn't matter his skin had scars and her curves had changed. They were the same here. Soul to soul. So he held her there, connected completely. So completely it didn't even bother him to feel the wetness of her tears on his shoulder. This was so big, so important, tears seemed vital.

"I love you," she whispered.

He said it back, for the first time without even an ounce of a twinge of guilt or regret, because she'd washed them away, with her love and forgiveness. All that was left in their wake was determination and surety.

So he moved, with slow, sure strokes, drawing her pleasure out with lazy patience. She chanted his name, rained kisses over his face, begged him for more, and still he kept a brutally easy pace.

Then she arched against him, scraping the lobe of his ear between her teeth. "All of you," she said, fingers digging into his arms. "I want all of you."

It unlocked that last piece of himself, and he gave her exactly what she asked for. All of him, every ounce of himself to her. Always and forever her.

They fell over that bright pulsing edge together, entwined tightly in each other. So tightly he was sure it took hours to unwind themselves from each other. Eternity to move off her, though he pulled her to him.

They lay there, breath slowing to normal, hearts eventually calming. And for the very first time in a very long time, he felt something like peace.

But they weren't ready for peace yet. Something evil still lurked out there, and they had to vanquish it before they could have their peace.

"I won't let anything happen to you, and you can get all prickly over that and go on about teamwork, but it doesn't change the simple truth I won't *let* anything happen to you."

She was quiet for a long moment, drawing gentle patterns across his chest. In the end, she didn't respond to that at all. She simply sighed. "I've missed you, Ty."

"I missed you, too, Jen." Never again would he let anything keep them apart that way. Not himself, and certainly not some maniac bent on terror.

JEN WILL DIE.

He wanted to carve those words into his skin, but he settled for the tree trunk. It was dark, a blackness that suited everything about his mood. Clouds had rolled in and not even the moon shone.

He couldn't see where he carved, but he carved the words anyway.

Jen will die.

Jen will die.

She'd let Ty touch her, and so she would die.

His hands cramped, and still he carved. Carved and carved trying to get rid of the need to carve the words into his own skin.

It would be her soon enough. The wait would have to be over.

At sunrise, his plan would begin.

Jen will die.

And Ty would watch.

Chapter Fifteen

Jen awoke the next morning with a contentment completely incongruous to the situation she found herself in.

She *knew* she should be worried and focused on the trouble at hand, but Ty's warm body next to her was everything she wanted, and the worry wouldn't win.

If there was anything she'd learned from the past year of troubles and fear for her family, it was that love endured. Hers and Ty's had endured all this time apart, and it would endure whatever danger the universe indiscriminately threw at them.

A few threatening notes and one arrow through a window were hardly going to take away this satisfied contentment, and that was that.

Her stomach growled, more than a little empty after she'd only picked at her dinner last night. She figured the numerous times they'd turned to each other in the night had burned off quite a few calories.

She looked at Ty's face in the dim glow of dawn filtering through the curtains. So strong and stern, even in sleep. It made her smile. It made her want to press her mouth to his. But her stomach was insistent and she figured Ty could use some extra sleep.

She slid out of bed and moved as quietly as possible for the door. The wind was rattling the cabin walls and it seemed to muffle the sound of her footsteps. She opened the door and peeked back at him. He didn't wake up, so she closed the door quietly behind her and went for the kitchen.

There was some bacon in the freezer she could defrost, along with some frozen hash browns she could fry up. She was in the mood for a deliciously filling, greasy breakfast and would be happy to putter about the kitchen for a bit. It would keep her mind occupied and her nerves settled.

She moved quietly around the kitchen, even let herself daydream about once this was all over. Would they spend the night at his place or hers? She couldn't imagine living above Rightful Claim, and not just because it would give her father a heart attack…but so would the alternative.

A Carson tramping around the apartment above the Delaney General Store. The thought made her smile.

A door creaked and she looked up, trying to hide her disappointment when it was Zach coming out of his bedroom door rather than Ty coming out of theirs.

He peered over at what she was doing. "You know you're an angel, right?"

She smiled at him. "An angel of fat."

"I'll take it. First I'm going to head out. One of the cameras is down. Could have been some animal interference, but I want to get it back up and running."

She frowned at Zach as he unlocked the door. "Don't you think you should wait? You shouldn't go out there alone."

"It's a typical malfunction." He held up his phone and tapped the screen. "I've got all the cameras tied in here, so I can look in all directions. I'll know if someone's out there before they know I am. Plus I'm carrying." He patted the gun at his hip. "You can watch me on the video on my computer in my room if you're nervous—I've got everything set up, you just have to walk in. Where's Ty?"

"Uh." He was still in her bed, fast asleep. Even though she wasn't embarrassed of being with Ty per se, it was a little awkward considering they were sharing a cabin with Zach. "He's, uh..." Her bedroom door opened and Ty stepped out, sleep rumpled and shirtless. "There."

"Ah." But Zach didn't say anything else. Just nodded his head and opened the door.

"Where are you going?"

"Jen'll fill you in." With that, he left and closed the door behind him.

Ty frowned, flipping the lock before turning to her. "He leaving us to our own devices?"

"A camera is down. He's going to check it out. Apparently he can see all the feeds on his phone and we shouldn't worry about it, but I don't like it."

"Me neither. I'll get dressed and head out there."

"I don't like that either," Jen muttered, but not loud enough for him to hear. She had no better ideas. Only dread creeping across all those places that had been happy and hopeful just a few moments before.

Ty returned, dressed in jeans and a T-shirt, boots on and laced. He'd fastened on his old Wild West–style holster that seemed more ominous than just part of his personal Carson style today.

"He said we can watch him on his computer. It's all set up. Maybe we should just do that?

Zach was an FBI agent. I feel like we should trust him a little."

"Shows what you know. FBI agents are a bunch of pencil pushers," Ty grumbled, but he strode for Zach's room instead of the door. Jen focused on breakfast prep as Ty returned with a laptop. He placed it on the kitchen table so she could see it out of the corner of her eye and he could sit at the table and watch.

On the screen were six boxes. Five of them showed areas around the cabin, but one was completely black.

"That must be the broken one," Ty murmured, sliding into a seat and watching the screen intently.

Then they were quiet, the only sounds Jen cooking up the hash browns and then the bacon. She plated breakfast, all daydreams lost to reality. When she slid into the seat next to Ty, they ate in continued silence, watching the screen of Zach's laptop. Occasionally Zach would appear in one box, then disappear.

The black screen popped back to life, showing a swath of trees moving with the wind.

"That's the view from the back of the cabin, right?" Jen asked. Though she'd lost her appetite to nerves, and now had a vague headache threatening at the base of her head, she forced herself to eat. She didn't want to admit that she was keeping her strength up in case they had to fight or run, but that was exactly the thought that prompted her to eat.

"Yeah, that's the one he fixed up on the roof. West corner." Ty chewed bacon thoughtfully. "I guess it could be as simple as the wind knocking it off. It's been blowing hard half the night."

"Zach said maybe animal interference."

Ty nodded. "That, too."

"It seems…far-fetched it'd be something that simple. That unthreatening."

Ty shrugged. "That's only because we're being threatened. Wind. Animals. Those things happen regardless of human threat."

She studied his profile. On the surface he seemed calm, but there was something about the way he ate. Mechanically, his eyes never drifting from the computer screen. "You're worried."

He flicked her a glance. "I'll worry about everything until this is over."

Yes, they both would. She turned her attention to the computer screen as well, and watched as Zach appeared and then disappeared again. "Maybe we should go out and tell him he fixed it."

"I think he knows. He's just checking the others."

The video flickered and all six sections of the

screen went black for a moment before coming back.

Ty narrowed his eyes, moved closer to study the screen. "That look different to you?"

It didn't, but the cold feeling seeping into her skin definitely didn't help matters. "Something isn't right."

"Yeah. You keep watching, I'll go out and check."

"Ty—"

But he held up a hand and pulled a key out of his pocket. He walked over to the couch, stuck the key in the small end table's drawer, and then pulled out her phone. "You keep watch and call or text me if you see anything on the screen I should watch out for."

"But if someone is out there, the ringer—"

He pulled out his phone. "I'll set it to vibrate."

"He could still hear—"

"Do you have a better idea?" Ty asked, and it wasn't laced with heat or derision. It was an honest question. "With Zach out there and something not right? I'm all ears, Jen, but I don't think we have time."

"Go. Be careful. Please."

He brushed a kiss over her cheek as he headed determinedly for the door. Jen didn't beg him to stay, though she wanted to. But she would be strong and she would be smart. She gripped her phone and watched all six boxes on the computer screen.

She was like the control tower. Much as it might feel like she was separate and doing nothing, she had an important function here.

So, she watched, waiting for Zach or Ty to appear. She frowned at the way the wind outside shrieked and made the entire house groan, then looked back at Zach's computer screen. Nothing moved. Not a tree, not a leaf, not a blade of grass.

Oh God. She jumped to her feet. Something was all wrong. She swiped open her phone and punched in Ty's number as she strode for the door.

It didn't ring. Nothing happened. She looked down at the screen. It was black. She hit the home button and tapped the screen, but nothing.

Her phone had died.

And Ty and Zach were out there and the cameras had been tampered with.

SOMETHING WAS OFF. The knowledge crept along Ty's skin as if he were walking through spider webs. But even when he checked his phone, there was no message from Jen so everything must be all right.

At least where the cameras were. There were spots the cameras didn't reach, so there could still be something wrong. Someone could be lurking, watching.

He walked carefully along the perimeter of the cabin, one hand on his phone and one on the handle of his gun in its holster. He watched the woods and saw nothing but the trees swinging wildly in the tempestuous wind.

Ty realized now, seeing the actual scene before him, that the video had been frozen. No wind. No movement. Which meant Jen wouldn't be able to warn him if anything bad was coming because there was no real-time video feed going to her.

He pulled the gun out of its holster, flicked off the safety and watched. By the time he'd made a full path around the cabin and stables, Zach was nowhere to be found.

Dread pooled, but Ty didn't let worry grow out of it. He'd figure this out, with skills honed from the army and the rangers. He could take on one unbalanced lunatic, and would. Because people's lives were in danger, and it was…

He couldn't allow the guilt anymore. Not with Jen's words and I love yous in his head, but he could say this was his *responsibility*. His purpose was to keep Jen safe. And to find Zach.

Ty might not have felt a particular affinity for Zach, but he wasn't about to let anyone, especially a blood relation, be hurt over something that had to do with him. Besides, maybe Zach was busy kicking butt on his own. Ty would only be backup.

He could hope.

He texted Jen first, tried not to consider how irritated she'd be.

Trouble. Stay put. Call Laurel.

He shoved his phone in his pocket. Jen wouldn't be able to see anything to help him unless the video unfroze, and he didn't consider that likely, but it was still a better shot than having her come out here. Inside the cabin she was safe.

Ty walked the perimeter again, this time making his circle bigger. He searched the trees, paused to listen and wished he'd brought his binoculars.

At one pause before he made it back to the front door again, he heard a rustle. He moved toward it carefully, pretended to veer off in the wrong direction. He did it a few more times, always keeping the location of the first rustle in his mind as he made a very circular path toward it.

He caught sight of something black and ducked behind a tree, but the color didn't move. Carefully, inching forward by avoiding as many dry leaves and twigs as he could, Ty moved toward the color.

The closer he got, the surer he was the figure was human. Zach. Seated on the ground, which wasn't right at all. Ty took another step closer and could see he wasn't just sitting there whiling away the time, he was tied to the tree, his head lolled down, blood dripping from a wound to his temple.

The spurt of fear and need to help had him speeding forward but halfway through the step his military training kicked in. It could be a trick. It could be—

The pain was so quick, so sharp, so absolutely blinding he could only fall with a strangled breath. He landed hard on the unforgiving ground, writhing in pain and trying to stop his body's natural reaction because he had to think.

But it hurt so damn bad thoughts wouldn't form. Knives in his foot, clawing through him. Searing, tearing pain.

But the image of Zach tied to the tree, bloody, flashed into his brain and he bore down to focus. He moved himself into a sitting position and looked down at his foot.

He was caught in a trap of some kind. He focused on his breathing over the panic. He had to keep his head, and he concentrated on the in and out of breathing, and helping Zach, as he eyed the metal clawed onto his foot.

If there was a bright side, and it was a pretty dim one, it was that he'd tripped it so quickly that his thick work boots had taken some of the trauma. Though the blade had sliced through flesh and potentially bone, he wasn't likely to bleed out like he might have if the trap had gotten more of his leg.

Then he heard more than a rustle. Footfall and twigs snapping. He realized he'd dropped his gun in the fall, but that didn't mean he was weaponless. He just had to move for a knife and—

"Tsk. Tsk." The man from Rightful Claim and Jen's store stepped forward, gun trained not on Ty—but on Zach. "And to think you were an army ranger. What an embarrassment."

Ty swallowed down the pain, the fear, and focused on the mission. Eliminating the threat. So, he flashed a grin. "Well, hi there, Braxton. It's about time."

ALL THAT WAS missing from this joyous scene was a chorus of angels. Everything—everything—had worked out. He almost wanted to cry, but instead he surveyed the man who had caused all his problems.

"Have you been waiting long?" he asked of

Ty. Ty's stoic response did nothing to irritate him. Oscar was also very good at appearing unmoved. It was a military thing.

Inside, Braxton *knew*, Ty was scared. In pain.

He studied the bear trap. It hadn't taken quite the chunk out of Ty he might have hoped, but Ty was stuck, and in pain. He wished it was more, but Ty's casual greeting couldn't hide the pale pallor to his face, or the grimace of pain.

It was better that Ty was only marginally hurt, and thus would not just live but stay conscious through what he had planned.

Yes, everything was better this way. He looked at the other man, still unconscious. Alive, but bleeding.

Braxton smiled. This was good. So good. In fact, he realized in this moment that Dr. Michaels had been wrong. So wrong she deserved the beating and stabbing he'd given her. Yes, he remembered it now. Every beautiful plunge into her fragile skin and hard bone.

He hadn't killed her, but he'd done irreparable damage.

It had been right all along. That violence. That payback.

He didn't need what Dr. Michaels had told him. Not focus. Not a *goal*.

He needed only blood.

So, without another word, Braxton walked away, whistling.

The next part of his plan was more blood, and it was already in place.

Chapter Sixteen

Jen had all the weapons she could find piled on the tabletop. Ignoring the way her arms shook, the way her head ached, she tried to figure different ways to carry as many guns and knives as possible on her person.

She refused to think about her dead phone, the dead landline she'd tried. She passed off the wave of dizziness that caught her as cowardly nerves and *refused* to give in to it.

She'd used Zach's computer to send an urgent email to Laurel, Cam, Grady and even the general email for the Bent County Sheriff's Department, but Zach's computer was so foreign to her she didn't have time to try to find an instant messaging service. She needed to protect herself, and she needed a plan.

A plan to protect the men out there trying to protect her.

Zach should be back by now, that was for

sure, and the fact Ty wasn't caused her to worry, but she wouldn't worry uselessly. She would act.

Once it was loaded, she shoved a smaller gun into the waistband of her jeans. She fixed a sheathed knife into the side of her boot. One rifle had a strap, so she set it aside, ready and loaded.

She had to steady herself on the table. The dizziness wouldn't go away and the painful throbbing in her head wouldn't stop. For a moment, she thought she'd be sick.

She took a deep breath to center herself. Ty was a former army ranger and Zach was a former FBI agent. There was no way she was going to have to go out there and save their butts. They were either perfectly fine, or taking care of everything.

She could stay where she was. Maybe she was really sick or something.

She shook that ridiculous thought away. She was letting emotional nerves turn into physical responses, and she wouldn't be that weak or cowardly.

She would take precautions, go outside and search for Zach and Ty, armed to the teeth, and hope to God Laurel read her email and sent someone to help them.

Even though she was probably overreacting.

If she found them out there, fine and in charge, she'd scold them both for scaring her to death.

And if they weren't, she'd fight for them the way they would fight for her. Maybe she wasn't as skilled, but she knew how to use a gun and she knew how to use her brain. Cowering inside wasn't acceptable. Not now.

Slowly, feeling sluggish and worse with every step, she hid the guns and knives she'd collected that she couldn't carry. But this time when she hid them, she put them places she would know where to get them. Places she might be able to reach if she needed to. Under couch cushions and under the sink in the bathroom.

More and more, she couldn't seem to think past the painful throbbing in her head. It was a heck of a time for her first migraine, but she wouldn't give in. Because Ty and Zach still weren't back and they should be.

They should be. So, even if things were fine, she had every right to be worried. To act. She gripped the table for a second, righting herself and breathing through the pain. She glanced at the computer screen, the six frozen boxes.

Except they weren't frozen anymore. Trees moved, grass swayed, and on one of the blocks, she saw two figures.

She swayed on her feet, nearly passed out, but it was Ty. Ty, caught in something. He couldn't seem to move his foot as he reached forward, fiddling with something around his foot. Zach was limp and clearly tied up. Since the feed was in black and white, she could only hope the smudge on his face was…anything except the blood it looked like it could be. Had to be if he was tied up.

No one showed up on any of the other screens, and Braxton or whoever had hurt them was nowhere to be seen. But they were hurt, and that made her decision.

She had to get to them. Save them. There was *no* choice. She slung the rifle over her shoulder and sprinted to the door. She fell forward, somehow grabbing onto the knob and keeping herself upright. She twisted, fought against the fog and the dizziness, then remembered she had to unlock the door.

It took too long to manage it. Why was fear making her so sluggish? Why couldn't she be strong and brave? She *had* to be. Zach and Ty were hurt and they needed her. She had to be brave.

She managed to twist the knob and push the door open.

To a man.

She screamed. Or thought she did. But the next thing she knew she was on the floor, looking up into Braxton Lynn's face. He looked the same as he had in her store, but it reminded her more of when he'd held the note up to her door than when he'd thanked her for the candy bar.

Something was missing in his eyes, something human. His pleasant smile was all wrong. She was on the floor. She had to reach for her gun, but her limbs were so heavy. So heavy. They didn't move.

"Oopsie," Braxton said cheerfully, nudging her legs out of the way of the door with his boot before he closed the door and flipped the lock. "Looks like someone has themselves a little carbon monoxide poisoning. Isn't that a shame?"

Poison. God, it all made sense now, even as the black crept through her mind and she lost her tenuous grasp on consciousness.

TY GRITTED HIS teeth against the pain, against the dull edge of shock trying to win. It couldn't. Zach was bleeding and Jen was on her own. Vulnerable and no doubt that madman was heading right toward her.

The way Braxton had simply studied the trap on Ty's foot, peered at Zach's limp body, then walked away, whistling, was all Ty needed to know to understand he was going for Jen now. That he didn't expect Ty or Zach to die. No, he wanted them alive for whatever was next.

Ty had to stop it. He had to escape this.

He'd tried to use whatever he could reach to pry the jaws of the trap open, but everything had broken off. He'd tried to pull the chain holding the trap down, but that had sent such a jolt of pain through him he'd almost passed out.

There had to be a way out of this. Had to be. He simply refused any scenario where he didn't free his foot and go save Jen.

Maybe she'd save herself. She was armed, and clearly stronger than Braxton gave her credit for if he thought the only thing that had kept her safe thus far had been him and Zach. Ty would believe Jen could handle herself, but he'd work like hell to get out of this and make sure she could.

He was about ready to test the give of the chain again when he heard a low sound. He wouldn't have thought it human, but Zach also moved a little, his head lolling, eyelids fluttering.

"Zach," Ty called. "Wake up. Now." They weren't too far apart, but Ty couldn't reach him. Could only watch as he still wavered somewhere just out of reach.

Ty wasn't about to give up on him. He kept talking, kept repeating Zach's name. "Zach. Come on, man. We need you now."

"Hurts," he mumbled. "Can't move."

"You're tied up to a tree. Some kind of head

injury. Braxton's got us stuck here and Jen's alone in the cabin. He's going to hurt her if we don't do something. You need to come out of it."

"Can't see. Black."

"Open your eyes," Ty commanded, trying to sound like an officer, not a desperate man shouting at an injured one.

It took another few minutes of talking him through it, repeating the situation over and over again, until Zach's eyes opened and stayed open. Finally, after what felt like eons, he seemed close to himself.

"We have to get out of this," Zach said, looking around the wooded area they'd found themselves in. "I want to believe Jen can take care of herself, but he took us both out."

"It's our own stupid faults. He wouldn't have if we'd stayed inside." Ty leaned forward, trying to reach the chain of the trap to tug at with his hands. If he could reach it, he could pull it off whatever it was attached to and maybe walk with the damn thing on his foot.

"No, he would have gotten us. I've dealt with enough criminals and unbalanced individuals to know he's determined, and he won't stop until he gets what he wants, or someone stops him."

"I'll stop him," Ty said, a swear, a promise.

"And me." Zach rolled his shoulders. "The knots aren't great and he didn't tie my legs. I can get out of it. I just…" Zach swore, twisting his body one way and then the other. Ty might have been impressed if steel claws weren't digging into his foot. "I can get out of it," Zach said more firmly this time. He maneuvered his body this way and that, grimacing and wincing, but never losing consciousness again.

"How long had I been out?" he asked, then hissed in pain.

"Too damn long."

"I don't remember how it happened."

Ty recognized the disgust of failure and guilt in Zach's tone and knew it wouldn't serve them any. "Well, since I currently have my foot caught in what appears to be a bear trap, I can't cast stones. He's gone after Jen. We've got to—"

Zach stood, the ropes falling to the ground.

"How the hell'd you do that, Houdini?"

"I told you the knots sucked. Now let's see what we've got here." He crouched in front of Ty's leg, squeezed his eyes shut for a second and swore a few more times. "Little bastard gave me a concussion."

"Let's give him a lot worse. Get me out of this thing."

It took too long, that much Ty knew. Like Ty, Zach used a variety of natural objects to try to pry the trap open.

"You should go."

Zach raised an eyebrow at Ty. "You want me to leave you here stuck in a nineteenth-century bear trap?"

"I've gotta believe Jen can ward off this guy, but I also believe two is better than one. Go. Help her and—"

Something clicked and the bear trap opened. It was almost as painful as the going in had been. His vision dimmed, but he focused on the hard ground beneath him and Zach's hand on his shoulder.

"Found the release mechanism. Can you walk?"

"Hell if I know. Let's find out." He took Zach's outstretched hand and got to his feet, putting pressure only on the good one. He had to have broken bones on top of the puncture wounds that were currently oozing blood.

"I could carry you."

Ty snorted. "You and what army? You've got a concussion and I'm not exactly a lightweight. Just give me an arm."

Zach did so, winding his arm around Ty, and Ty did the same. He took a tentative step with it, not putting full weight on. His good leg nearly buckled, but Zach kept him upright.

It would have to do. They moved slowly, and Ty swore, repeatedly, with every step of his injured foot, but kept stepping forward with

Zach's help. "Toward the cabin," he said with gritted teeth.

"You aren't going to be much help."

Ty pointed to the gun that had fallen when the trap had gotten him. "The hell I'm not."

Zach bent to pick it up as Ty balanced on one foot. Ty took it from him and shoved it in its holster. "You got your phone on you?"

"No. He's got it. You?"

Ty paused. Much as it galled him to waste time, he pulled his phone out of his pocket and hit Laurel's number. He motioned Zach for them to keep walking as he used his free hand to hold the phone to his ear.

"T—"

He didn't even let her get his name out. "Get as many deputies up here as you can. Plus Grady and Noah." Cursing his bad luck, he added, "And Dylan and Cam. Everybody. Anybody."

"They're already on their way. We got an email from Jen. I tried to call but her phone goes straight to voice mail and the cabin phone line is dead. We've got some car trouble, but we're working on it. Someone should be there in ten minutes. You don't sound so good."

"Minor injuries. Have an ambulance ready, but don't send it up here yet."

"Is Jen okay?" Laurel demanded. Since Ty didn't know how to answer that, he didn't.

"Gotta focus." He hit End and shoved his phone in his pocket. "Cavalry's coming," he said through gritted teeth.

"Good. I've got a bad feeling we're going to need it. We've still got a ways to go."

Too much of a ways. "Go ahead."

"How are you going to—"

He leaned against a tree and handed the gun to Zach. "You run hard as you can. I'll be behind you. Just make sure she's safe. Help her if she's not. We don't have the time for me."

Zach nodded once. "I'll see what I can do." Then he was off.

It about killed Ty to watch Zach run off, knowing Jen's fate was in his hands. No. Her own hands and Zach's hands and all the help they had coming.

He didn't even consider waiting. He braced himself, then took off after Zach in the fastest limping job he could manage. Maybe he wouldn't save the day, but he wasn't going to take the chance that he wouldn't need to.

He'd do whatever he could, fight through any pain, suffer any consequences to be sure Jen was safe.

IT WAS FREEZING in the cabin, even with the fire crackling in the hearth. The windows were open since he had to air out all that carbon monoxide he'd poured inside. He'd gotten a bit of a headache himself when he put the straitjacket on Jen.

And everyone said his odd collection of things would be a waste.

He laughed, pleased all over again at the genius. He wished he'd thought of the carbon dioxide sooner. It would have saved him some trouble.

But he'd been able to use his bear trap. Ty's blood was on it now. Worth it. Everything was worth blood.

Jen moaned, moving weakly against the straitjacket that tied her arms behind her and her body to the couch. He watched her slowly drift to consciousness from his position by the window, breathing in fresh air.

He wanted to watch the fear creep into her. Wanted to see the panic on her face when she realized where she was. When she realized he'd immobilized her completely. When she realized no one could or would help her now because he was the only one here.

He laughed again, and her eyes flew open. Pretty eyes. Such a shame to squeeze until they popped right out.

Would that be bloody? Hmm.

He thought for a second about focus, about goals, about what Dr. Michaels had always told him.

But she'd been wrong. Leaning into the black was so much better. Hadn't everything gotten better since he'd stabbed the good doctor? Once he was done with Ty, he'd go back and finish the job.

Revenge. It wasn't just for Oscar anymore, and though a part of him felt guilty, a part of him was too excited about what was to come.

Blood. Blood. Blood. Ty's suffering would be for Oscar. Jen's blood would be for him.

Her eyes darted around the room as she swallowed and moved, trying to escape the straitjacket. She wouldn't be able to, but it'd be fun to watch her try. Fun to watch her scream and beg.

He'd watch for as long as that thrilled him, then he'd kill her. Just like Dr. Michaels, but he'd finish the job. Leave her ripped apart and bloody for Ty to find.

He frowned a little. It would be possible someone else would find her first, and that wouldn't do. No, Ty had to be the one who stepped into all the glorious blood he'd soon shed.

He still had some work to do to perfect his plan.

He watched her struggle against the bonds he'd put on her, and smiled. He'd have the perfect view to do just that.

Chapter Seventeen

Jen pretended to slip back into unconsciousness so she could think. She tried to remember what had happened or how she'd ended up immobile on the couch.

Her arms were wrapped uncomfortably around her body, but she couldn't move out of the position. It was like she was tied together, fastened to the couch.

Panic came, though she tried to fight it. She wanted to pretend like she was still unconscious but she just…she couldn't. She writhed and tried to free her hands, move her arms only a little, but she couldn't.

She sobbed out a breath, was afraid she wouldn't be able to suck in another. She opened her eyes as she desperately tried to move her limbs. What had he done to her? Why couldn't she move even her arms?

She blinked once, then twice, thought maybe

she was hallucinating before she came to the conclusion that her eyes were not deceiving her.

He'd put her in an honest-to-goodness strait-jacket.

"Worked out that it fit almost perfectly."

She jerked at his voice, even though she knew he'd been there. It wasn't that he spoke that gave her a start, it was how...conversational he sounded.

"One of my foster mothers used to put me in it. I kept it. A token of the time."

"That's horrible," Jen replied. Talking helped ease some of her panic. If she could focus on Braxton, on talking, she could take her mind off the fact that she couldn't move.

"It was horrible. And now it's horrible for you."

"Th-that doesn't seem very f-fair," Jen managed. She tried to ignore the fact she couldn't move. Because she had to be able to get out of this, or at least stall...whatever he was going to do to her. The longer she could keep him from hurting her, the better shot she had of someone coming to save her. Them.

God. Ty. Zach. They were all tied up in some fashion or another now. She didn't understand how one lone, crazy man had been able to best all three of them.

Except no. He hadn't bested them yet. She

had to believe there was a way out of this. As long as she believed, there was a chance.

"Fair?" He laughed, and there was no edge or bitterness to the sound. He seemed genuinely amused. "You don't actually think life is *fair*, do you?"

She wouldn't answer that—not with the awful joyful gleam in his ice-blue eyes. "I-it's Braxton, right? You're Braxton."

He tilted his head and studied her. "Are we going to be friends now, Jen? You were nice enough to give me a candy bar, right? You're going to be nice enough to talk to me. Soften me up and maybe I'll let you go."

She closed her eyes and breathed. She thought about Ty. If he were in her place, he wouldn't panic. He wouldn't cry. Sure, he had military training she didn't, but she could be as tough as him when push came to shove. When she had to be.

"I know you're going to hurt me because you think it'll hurt Ty, but—"

He laughed again, louder, but it had an edge to it now that had her swallowing at the lump in her throat.

"Now you're going to lie to me?" he demanded, still standing over by the window. "You're going to lie there, in a *straitjacket*, and tell me Ty doesn't care about you. Oh, Jen, you're stupider than I gave you credit for. You think I don't know you let him touch you? You think I don't know everything that went on in that room last night?"

Horror waved through her, a crawling sensation of disgust crept along her skin as he pointed to the bedroom she'd shared with Ty.

"You..."

"Amazing what you can learn from watching people on video. Your third wheel friend knows that, doesn't he? Don't worry. It was dark. I couldn't really see anything, but I know what you did. I know what you said. Love is such a powerful motivator, don't you think? When you love someone, you want to hurt the people who hurt them."

"No. You want to heal the hurt in them, not punish the person who hurt them."

Braxton laughed bitterly. "Oh, aren't you full of it."

"No, I'm not." Was she really arguing with a homicidal maniac? It was probably pointless and stupid, but it kept her attention off the horrible sensation of forced immobility. "If someone hurt Ty, I would want to help Ty, not worry about stupid, selfish revenge."

"Stupid?" he repeated in a low, dangerous tone. "Selfish?"

"Yes, stupid. And selfish on both parts. I

would want him okay, not someone else hurt. And Ty would never want me to hurt people *for* him. If he had a problem, he'd deal with it himself. I know you're trying to… You think this means you cared about your brother—"

"Cared?" He almost screamed the word but then he seemed to shake himself. He turned away from her, muttering something she couldn't hear. Then he repeated her words, till he was just muttering the word *himself* over and over again. As if he was working out a math problem, but every word he uttered was simply *himself*.

"You've given me an idea, Jen." He turned back to her, affable and pleasant again. "An interesting idea. Do you think Ty would sacrifice his own life for yours? Or would he hurt you to save his own skin? Which one's love?"

Without knowing what Braxton was planning, thinking, she didn't want to give him any answer. So she simply swallowed.

Braxton finally moved away from the window, but he moved toward her and that was when she realized he had a very large knife in his hand.

"Do knives make you nervous, Jen?" he asked, sounding almost concerned, almost human. He twisted the knife one way and then another. When he knelt next to the couch, she whimpered no matter how she tried not to make a noise.

Braxton smiled, brandishing the knife above her head. "You're terrified. My, my. I quite like them. Anything sharp really. Blood is so…interesting. So soothing. Would Ty shed his own to save you yours?"

A tear slipped over. She could feel it trail down her cheek. Braxton pointed the sharp tip of the knife at it. She squeezed her eyes shut as the tip of the knife touched the teardrop and pierced her skin. It hurt, but she couldn't move. She was stuck, the tip of the blade cutting into her skin.

"Blood and tears." He made a considering noise, but the knife eased off her cheek. She felt something trickle down her chin—tears or blood or both—and tried to believe she would survive this.

But she didn't have any idea how.

THE CABIN CAME into view, and with it, Zach standing behind the stables. Ty's body was becoming slowly numb. He welcomed it, as long as it didn't interfere with his ability to move forward.

"He's got the windows open," Zach said by way of greeting.

Ty glared at Zach when he finally reached him. "Then get in there and—"

"I scoped it out. We need to work this together. I go in guns blazing, not only do I end up dead, but she might, too. We'll have to find a way to draw him out."

"The concussed and the mangled foot?"

"If it's all we got. I'd like to wait for the cops."

Fury, fear and sheer frustration welled up inside Ty like a tidal wave destroying all the numb. "Wait for… Are you—"

"I said I'd like to, not that I would." Zach scanned the trees, calm and sure. Ty might have been reassured if he wasn't so scared. "What's taking them so long?"

Ty tried not to think about all the worst-case scenarios. The wind having knocked down trees to block the road, Braxton having men working for him, happily picking off cops as they came.

He couldn't think about it now. He had to get to Jen. "What's the situation inside?"

Zach eyed him and Ty knew in a moment it was terrible, but before he could start forward, Zach spoke in clear, concise military tones.

"She's tied up. I need you to be prepared for that. He's got the door booby-trapped, but the windows are open. I don't see any traps, but I've got to believe he's got something going on there. He's bested us once, so we can't let him do it again. We have to be more careful than we were. Smarter."

"Tied up where? How?"

Zach scrubbed a hand over his face, smearing some of the blood across his cheek accidentally. "On the couch. I can't be sure, but I think he's got her in a straitjacket."

Ty swore and moved forward, but Zach grabbed his arm again, this time giving it a good yank.

"You're not new to this," he snapped, his voice firm. "You know dangerous situations, and people who would do anything to prove their point. You know the dangers and everything that could go wrong. You have to forget it's Jen for right now."

"That's bull. Why did I do all those things in the army? Because they were supposed to keep the people I loved here safe. Why'd you get kicked out of the FBI, Zach? Because you cared about your family more than you cared about procedure. So, don't give me that crap right now."

"I'm not talking about arbitrary procedure. I'm talking about a plan that prioritizes getting Jen out of there without getting anyone hurt."

"I'll get hurt. Ten times over." He'd go to hell and back and enjoy the ride.

"You think she'd want that?"

"I think I don't care." But it poked at some of his certainty. She wouldn't want that. It'd hurt her, and that was the last thing Ty wanted. She was already being hurt, far too much. His fault, and his guilt was talking. She wouldn't want that either. "What kind of booby traps?"

"The door's got some kind of trip wire. My instinct is explosives. Potentially enough to blow this whole clearing to hell."

Ty fought the fatigue and pain going on inside his body to think. *Think.* Jen had tried to understand Braxton, tried to understand his emotions. She'd been right, and he needed to think like she had.

"He incapacitated us, but didn't kill us," Ty said. "He could have. Easily."

"Yeah."

"He wants to torture Jen, but he wants me alive to see it. Whatever trap he's got going on in there isn't big scale because that'd ruin it. End it. He wants me to suffer—if we all die, I don't suffer."

"Okay. Okay. I'll give you that. But two things we have to keep in mind. First, I don't think he cares if *he* gets hurt as long as he gets revenge, so that's not a threat to him. Second, if you go in there, he hurts Jen. The closer you are to her with him the more likely he is to do something to her."

Zach was right. It burned, but Zach was right. The minute Ty stepped foot in that cabin, Jen was in at least twice as much danger. Which meant he had to do something that went against every fiber of his being.

He had to trust someone else with Jen's safety. He had to put it all in someone else's hands. He had to trust, and he had to believe, in someone aside from himself—not just Zach, but Jen, too.

Guilt told him this was all his fault and he should take responsibility for it. Guilt told him he couldn't let Zach get even more hurt when this was Ty's own fight.

But Jen… Here, in that cabin, she'd forgiven him everything—his faults, his choices, the things he'd done or not done. Everything he'd hated himself for, she'd washed away with forgiveness. And she always had.

She'd told him to let it go, to forgive himself, and he had tried, or had believed he might someday. But in this moment, he had to. Because if he didn't, Jen would more than likely die.

"You'll go in," Ty said, having no trouble snapping into army ranger mode. "There's a secret passageway on the opposite side of the cabin, but it's been sealed. Still, with the right timing, the right tools, you can either unseal it or create enough noise he comes out."

Zach nodded.

"If I situate myself in the hayloft, I've got the perfect position to pick him off if he comes out the door."

Zach rose an eyebrow and nodded toward Ty's foot. "How you going to get up there?"

"Carefully," Ty replied. Zach held out the gun Ty had given him and Ty took it. "You'll be unarmed."

"You're better off with the gun. You can pick him off through a window, we end this. Besides, he took my gun and my phone, but I've still got my knife." Zach motioned to his boot. "Vanessa gave me that idea."

"Thank God for Vanessa and her arsenal. Let's go." He motioned Zach to follow him back into the woods. Zach offered an arm, but Ty shook his head. Walking hurt like nothing he'd ever experienced, but Jen's life hung in the balance. He'd deal.

They moved through the cover of the trees to the opposite side of the cabin. Braxton couldn't know he was out here and free, or Jen and Zach were in even more danger.

Ty moved up the side of the cabin and showed Zach the secret passage and where it had been sealed.

Zach pulled out the knife. "This should do

the trick. If not, I'll start banging away, try to lure him out."

Ty nodded. "I doubt he knows who you are, so hurting Jen to get to you won't matter to him, hopefully. He might think you're of some emotional connection to me, though. He might even know you're my cousin, my blood. So he could hurt you again, to get to me. We can't discount that."

"Yeah, I haven't let a man best me twice in this lifetime. I don't plan to start now."

"That's the Carson spirit." Ty studied the clearing, the cabin. "I'll be in the hayloft, out of sight, but if you get him out the front door, I can take him out. Jen's the priority."

Zach nodded, already prying at the seal on the door. "You should get out of sight now. I'll see what I can do here, but no matter what, I'll get her out. That's a promise."

Like Jen had chosen to forgive him, love him, Ty chose to believe Zach. He clapped him on the shoulder. "Take care of yourself, cousin." And then he limped for the stables, gun at the ready.

BLOOD AND TEARS, but Ty wasn't here. Should he kill her and then bring Ty to the aftermath? Better for him to watch. He'd get the blood, and the revenge. Oscar wanted the revenge. He wanted the blood.

But she was right there and all it would take was a few minutes. He could cut her to ribbons and it would be done. Right now. No more waiting.

Why did he have to wait?

"Braxton, I know you want to hurt me..."

Her voice was so sweet he wished she'd stop talking. It wasn't like the doctor's voice. The doctor had always been so cold. So condescending. Jen sounded afraid of him.

He liked that.

"Could you let me out of this thing? I don't care if you tie me up again. I just can't lie like this."

He walked back over to her. She wanted out, and maybe that would suit his purposes. Maybe a little fight would make this all sit right. He'd had to fight the doctor. Element of surprise, yes, but she'd tried to push him off.

He'd liked that. The way she'd hit and begged and still he'd plunged the knife into her skin.

His stomach jumped with anticipation, even more so when Jen's fear shone in her eyes like tears.

"You want out?"

She swallowed visibly. "Just a little? I know you have to keep me tied up, but if I could just move a little. My circulation and I... I..."

Desperation. He liked it on her. Fear and

desperation. It was what he wanted from Ty, but maybe he'd practice on sweet Jen. He held the knife over her head again, watched as she squeezed her eyes shut and braced herself for another cut.

The one from before was just a little dot now, a little smear of blood and tears down her cheek and chin.

Pleasure spurted through him, dark and wonderful. If only this moment could last.

"Cut yourself," he said.

"What?"

He liked the way she paled. Fear. He liked her fear so much. It was better than a shot of whiskey. Better than the drugs Oscar had liked so much that Braxton had never understood.

Why do drugs when you could make someone afraid? When the power of that could stir everything inside you?

"I'll free one arm. If you take the knife and cut yourself. More than I did on your face." He wondered if it would be more or less satisfying to watch her cause herself pain, or if it would be better for him to do it. Her hurting herself would cause Ty more pain, he thought, but the blood on her face made him wonder if he cared. "Maybe your wrist. It'd take a while for one wrist to bleed out."

"But..."

"One wrist. Then I decide if I do the rest, or you do. One wrist. Then we get Ty. I'd like to get a better look at Ty's blood, too. Maybe so would you."

"Braxton—"

He laid the flat of the blade against her cheek. "Sweet Jen didn't do anything to deserve this, but you love a monster. Maybe you're a monster, too. Monsters need to bleed, Jen. Isn't that what all the fairy tales tell us?"

But she didn't answer. She only cried.

Chapter Eighteen

Jen would scold herself for crying later. For now, it was the release of fear she'd needed to center herself. "Okay, Braxton," she said, opening her eyes and making sure to look at him, to try to be a person to him. "I'll cut my wrist if you let me have one arm."

One arm would be all she'd need. There was a pistol in the cushion of the couch, unless he'd found it when she'd been unconscious. But she'd take the chance—had to.

Zach and Ty were stuck and she had to be able to save herself, and them.

Braxton could hurt her, *would* hurt her, but as long as he didn't kill her she had a shot. And he wouldn't kill her as long as Ty was somewhere else, so there was some bright side to his being stuck.

She just needed to get to that gun, and she just needed it to be there. One arm. All she needed was one arm. Didn't matter if she had to cut herself to do it.

She breathed in and out, trying to accept the fact she would have to do it. She'd have to cut her own flesh and…

She had to convince him to free her arm first. She had to actually get him to do it before she worried about pressing a sharp blade to her wrist.

An involuntary shudder moved through her, but she forced herself to look at Braxton and tried to treat him like a human being even though whatever made someone humane was clearly missing in him.

"I've killed before, Jen, you know," he said, so simply, so *conversationally* the way you'd tell someone you didn't care for pizza. He stared at her intently, looking for a reaction.

She didn't know what kind he wanted. If she did, she'd act it out and give it to him. She'd go along with whatever he wanted. "I'm sorry," she whispered.

"Sorry?"

It wasn't the answer he wanted, but what was? What could she say to just make him untie her?

No time for panic. Breathe in. Breathe out. As long as Ty isn't here, you have time.

But did Ty have time? Did Zach?

She couldn't think about them.

"Are you going to let me go? Please? I'm going to have a panic attack."

He laid the flat of his blade against her cheek like he'd done before, and again she couldn't hide her response. A shudder, a wince and more tears welling behind her eyelids.

She opened her eyes when he did nothing. He was grinning. Finally, it started to make sense. He wanted her to be afraid. He wanted her to shudder and wince at the idea of his killing people, over the idea and possibility he could kill her.

"Panic attack. I might like to watch that."

He was never going to let her go. He was going to torture her until… When?

"But I'd like to see your blood more," he continued. He pressed the knife against her cheek until she hissed out a breath when it lightly scored her chin.

He leaned in closer, his face so close to hers she could feel his breath against the blood dripping down her neck.

"Please let me out," she whispered, letting her fear and her tears run free, since that's what he wanted from her anyway. Fear and tears and blood. "Please. I just need to sit up or move my arm. Please. Anything."

He didn't lean away, though he did pull the

knife off her skin. But then he replaced it with something much worse.

His tongue.

A groan mixed with a scream tore from her throat as she struggled to move her face, her body, her entire being away from him as he licked the blood off her face.

But he only made a considering noise, as if he was mulling over the taste of her blood.

Shudders racked her body and true fear crept through everything. She didn't know how to fight insanity. She didn't know how to escape. A tiny part of her wondered if death wouldn't just be easier.

The thought passed. Ty was out there, trapped. Zach was trapped and probably hurt. Her entire family was trying to solve the mystery of Braxton Lynn. Someone would make it here eventually and help her.

Ty was counting on her. He'd left her alone thinking she could handle anything that came her way, so she would. She *would*.

If she believed that, she could endure anything.

Anything.

"Please, Braxton. Just a break from the straitjacket. Besides, if you take all this fabric off you'll be able to cut me wherever you want."

"I want to watch you cut yourself, Jen. A test.

Which do I like better? Inflicting pain? Or making you inflict pain on yourself? I get blood either way."

"Then just free my arms. Please. *Please.*"

He sighed heavily. "Fine. But only because I want the experiment. It's important to find out what makes you feel the best, isn't it?" He undid some strap, then rolled her to the side so her back was to him. "I thought I liked revenge. Doing something for my brother. Ty was supposed to be Oscar's brother, but he ratted him out. Did you know that about the man you let touch you? That he's no better than a cowardly tattletale?"

She bit her tongue against the need to defend Ty. He wanted her fear and her desperation, but she doubted he'd care for her anger.

There were sounds, the gradual loosening of the fabric holding her arms around her. She nearly wept with relief, but then Braxton paused.

"If you try anything, this is my plan. Cut you to ribbons. Bathe this room in your blood. Then bring Ty in to see your mangled corpse that he should have been brave enough and smart enough to save. One attempt at escape, one look at the door, one wrong move—you're dead, and he sees it *all.*"

She didn't suppress this shudder since she knew he liked it. If she gave him everything he liked, maybe he'd make a mistake—get too excited. No matter what, as long as she did what he said, he'd keep her alive. She wouldn't be the sacrifice he made to hurt Ty.

Braxton pushed her up into a sitting position. He held the strap of one arm tight around his fist. He tugged the other sleeve off. "I'm going to give you the knife. You're going to slice your wrist. If you do all that, I won't put the straitjacket back on."

Jen nodded, and her arm that was now free shook. Even if she could muster up the guts or strength to cut herself, she wasn't sure her limbs would cooperate. Still, Braxton slowly pressed the handle of the knife into her palm—holding her other arm still by the straps on the jacket.

With his hand now free, he pulled a gun out of his pocket. Everything inside her sank. It was the gun she'd hidden in the couch.

"Hope you weren't planning on using this." He smiled indulgently.

She shook her head even though that's exactly what her plan had been. Still, he'd given her a knife. Maybe he had the gun pointed at her, but she had a weapon, too. If he let go of her other arm, she could knock him down.

She just needed the right moment.

But he just kept smiling, like he knew every move she'd make and had a counterplan for it.

He didn't take the straitjacket off her completely. Instead, he pushed the sleeve still on her arm up, revealing her wrist and adjusting his hold onto her forearm.

"Cut yourself. And don't wimp out. A real cut. I want to see blood *gush*. I like knives better, but if I have to shoot you to get blood, I'll do it. So, pick your poison."

Jen briefly considered letting him shoot her. It might be better for her in the long run. But she had a knife now. He'd untied her. Her feet were still fastened together, but she had a weapon and she wasn't tethered to the couch any longer.

"Go on now."

She nodded, arms still shaking as she slowly brought the knife to where he held her wrist out for her. She'd only have to lunge forward, right in the gut. He'd shoot her, but he'd be hurt, too. Wouldn't it be worth it?

"Do it now," Braxton ordered, jerking her wrist toward the knife. "Or I'll put you back in. I'll carve that pretty face of yours all up while your arms are tied around you. Would you prefer that, Jen?"

No, she wouldn't, but she was afraid he was going to do it anyway. But first, she'd cut herself. It excited him, and if he leaned down to lick her wrist like he'd done with her face, she'd have the best chance to stab him where it would do the most damage.

She closed her eyes and pressed the blade to her wrist, inhaling sharply to give herself one last second before she inflicted pain.

But then she heard something. Like a door being opened somewhere. She kept her eyes closed, even as hope soared through her. She had to cut herself and keep Braxton's attention.

"What the hell was that?" Braxton demanded as she opened her eyes.

He not only looked away, he turned, which gave her the opportunity to strike.

A SCREAM TORE through the air. Ty immediately jumped from the hayloft. He saw stars, the pain in his foot so bright and burning he nearly lost consciousness.

When a gunshot sounded, Ty didn't care about the pain. He ran.

He stopped for a moment at the window, but he couldn't see anything. It'd have to be the door—regardless of booby traps.

Zach was reaching the door just as Ty rounded the corner.

"Was just about in when I heard it. I'll kick in the door. Stay to the side. We'll give it a minute, me in first since I've got two good feet, then you follow and shoot."

Ty nodded.

Zach reared back and kicked. It didn't open the door, but it jarred it, so Zach kicked again. This time it splintered, and opened weakly.

Almost immediately there was another gunshot.

They both swore, but there was no time to consider the ramifications of Braxton's shooting at them. Zach went in first, a low roll that hopefully got him some cover. Ty moved in, weapon drawn.

Braxton stood behind the couch, his arm wrapped around Jen's throat. She was limp and lifeless, blood smeared all over her face. Braxton held the barrel of the gun to her head and grinned.

Jen was too close for comfort, but they simply didn't have another option. Ty aimed and fired.

Braxton jerked back and Jen fell to the floor. Zach and Ty moved forward as a unit. Red bloomed on Braxton's shirt and he touched the wound and smiled. "Look at all that blood," he murmured, transfixed by the sight of his own fingers drenched in his own blood.

Then his eyes rolled back and he collapsed in a heap. Ty didn't think he was dead—he'd probably just passed out.

"I'll tie him up," Zach said.

Ty tossed him his phone. "Call Laurel again and find out what the damn holdup is. We need that ambulance." He looked down at Jen. Her face was covered in blood and she was so pale and lifeless everything inside him went cold. He fell to his knees next to her and nearly wept when her eyes fluttered open.

"You're okay," she murmured.

"Where are you bleeding, darling?" She tried to move, but he stopped her, afraid she'd hurt herself more. "I don't see where you're bleeding from."

"He smeared it all over me. He…" She shuddered, closing her eyes again. "S'okay, though. Have to."

"Have to *what*?"

"Get shot. It's like… It's like. Laurel and Cam and Dylan, they all did."

"Baby, shh. Just tell me where—"

"But then it'll be okay, right? Because they did, but now it's good. We'll be good, because I got shot. It's the answer to the curse. It'll be okay."

She wasn't making any sense, but he didn't care. "Yeah, it'll be okay. It has to be." It had to be. With shaking hands, he moved his fingers over her, trying to find the wound. It had to be on her back, but he was loath to turn her over. But there was bleeding that had to be stopped.

"My arm," she mumbled. "Hurts. Under my arm."

He didn't know which one she was talking about, so gently he lifted the one closest to him, but she shook her head sluggishly.

He lifted the other one, found the bleeding, gaping wound right under her armpit. Not fatal, thank God, but they needed to stop the bleeding. Get her safe.

"Stabbed him, but he shot me."

Ty nearly wept right there, but he held it together and took the first aid kit Zach handed him.

"We have to get her to a hospital," he said, opening the case and pulling out all the bandages inside. He handed half to Zach to start unwrapping.

"How? On your bike?"

Ty shook his head, pressing the first pad of gauze to her wound. She hissed out a breath, but her eyes remained closed and her breathing was getting too shallow for his comfort. "What did Laurel say?"

"Trees down everywhere. Their cars were tampered with. The ambulance is trying to get up here, but without a road—"

"We'll carry her to it, then." Ty wrapped more

bandages, as many as he could manage, as tight as he could manage, around her arm.

"I don't know if you recall the fact your foot is torn to hell."

"You'll carry, then. We have to get her to that ambulance. We'll bandage her up and get her out of here."

"What about him?"

Ty didn't even glance back at Braxton's body. "He can rot in hell."

Chapter Nineteen

"I convinced him to let my arms free."

"How did you do that?" Thomas asked gently.

Jen sat in the hospital bed, tired and a little off from the drugs they'd given her, but she'd felt up to giving her statement to the police. She wanted to get it all out and over with, before the nurses let her family back in, before she saw Ty.

She wanted to get rid of all the ugliness so it could be behind her. "He told me he'd let my arms loose if I cut myself for him."

Thomas raised an eyebrow as he wrote that down on his notepad.

"He was obsessed with blood. He seemed to lose his grasp on reality or humanity with every passing moment. The need for revenge against Ty sort of faded into…bloodlust I guess." She shuddered again, was pretty sure she'd flash back to Braxton whenever she saw blood.

But she was alive and Braxton… "Thomas, is Braxton…"

"He made it to the hospital, but he'd lost too much blood."

"Braxton said..." She swallowed against the wave of nausea—didn't know if it had to do with the drugs or everything else. "He said he'd killed people."

Thomas nodded solemnly. "Laurel's been in touch with the authorities in Arizona. They've been able to connect him to an attack on his therapist, along with a murder of one of Oscar Villanueva's victims."

She slumped in her bed, far too aware that she could have easily been another of his murder victims.

"Do you want to stop for now? I can come back—"

"No. I want it over with."

"All right. So, he untied you?"

"Yes, and then there was this noise and I took the moment of distraction to stab him, but he had a gun and he shot me. I'm not sure he meant to, it was more of an impulse response. I mean, he wanted to hurt me, but I don't think he wanted to kill me yet. But things get fuzzy from there."

"You don't remember Zach and Ty coming in?"

"No. No, it just kind of goes blank. I remember talking to Ty in the cabin. He was trying to figure out how I was hurt. Will Ty be in trouble, since I can't remember?"

"No. We have Zach's statement, cut-and-dried self-defense. Ty will be fine."

Jen nodded, closing her eyes against the fatigue.

"You should rest, Jen. I've got enough to build the case and file everything. I may need to ask you a few more questions in the future, depending on how everything goes, but we're mostly done."

Jen grimaced but she nodded. "All right." She tried to smile. "Thank you."

Thomas paused on his way out of the hospital room. "I'm… I wish we could have done more."

Jen shook her head and sighed. "You did what you could. We all did. And now it's over."

Thomas nodded and slipped out the door. Jen allowed herself a moment of quiet, of release. They'd all done the best they could, and now it was over. Everyone she loved was safe, and she'd survived.

Everything was going to be okay.

It was an emotional acceptance because there had been a moment there, before she'd managed to convince him to take the straitjacket off, and for a second there after he'd shot her, where she'd been certain she was going to die.

But she was alive.

She heard the door swish open, and opened her eyes to see Ty. He had a crutch under one arm, and a medical boot on the foot.

She hadn't seen him since the ambulance, and she'd been in and out at that point. But he'd held her hand the whole way to the hospital.

"You should've told Hart to scram."

She held out her good arm to him. "I wanted it over. Did you sneak back here or are you allowed?"

He managed a smile. "Which do you think?" He moved over to her, relying on the crutch. She scooted to the side of the bed so he could slide onto it next to her.

They didn't say anything else. He just wrapped his arms around her and she leaned into the strong wall of his chest.

She thought she might cry, but she didn't. Instead, she just breathed. It was over, and she had this. Everything was okay.

She hadn't realized she'd said it out loud until Ty spoke.

"Yeah it is," he said before kissing her temple. "You know when they'll spring you?"

"Tomorrow they said. They didn't let you out already?"

"Discharged and all." He fidgeted irritably. "I'll have to have some surgery later, but they want some of the wounds to heal first."

"Not everyone can say they have a limp because of a bear trap."

"Making jokes already? I'm impressed, darling." He kissed her again, and his grip on her never loosened.

"I don't want to think about horrible things, or be angry or sad or scared for at least a month."

"Let's shoot for a year."

"Maybe two."

He laughed, but then he just held her, so she held him back. "It really is okay," she whispered. "And there's a lot of okay left to get."

"I know. It's going to take me a little while to… Hell, I thought you were dead, Jen."

She pressed her forehead into his neck. "But I'm not. Which means we have a lot of plans to make. So, you think on that."

The door opened again, and her whole family poured in. A nurse started mounting objections, but Grady easily sweet-talked her out of the room.

Hilly rushed over and gave her a hug, while Dylan insisted Vanessa take a seat. Zach hovered in the background, but Jen motioned him over.

"Glad you're okay, Jen," he offered.

She gently touched the bandage on his temple. "Thank you for everything."

He shrugged, clearly uncomfortable, and then

he quickly moved away as her father came over and gave her a hug. Laurel perched herself on the little sliver of bed at the end.

"Well, here we are again," Jen said, opting for cheerful. "But you know, it's over now. We all got shot, and we'll all get our happily-ever-afters."

"Oh, for heaven's sake," Laurel muttered. "There's *no curse*."

"Not anymore," Jen agreed, grinning when Laurel rolled her eyes.

"What about Zach?" Hilly asked. "He's a Carson."

"I'm a Simmons," Zach replied firmly.

"No, Hilly's right. Zach's one of us," Grady replied. "But we're out of Delaneys for him to pair up with."

"Eh, you never know when one will pop out of the woodwork," Vanessa returned with a grin. "Watch your back, Zach."

He scoffed, but Jen rather liked the idea. And she liked having everyone around, talking as if things were normal. As if she wasn't hooked up to a hospital bed, as if nothing had terrorized any of them over the course of the past year.

It was nice. It was...perfect really. A cleansing moment to put everything about yesterday behind her.

She tried to hide the yawns, the exhaustion,

but pretty soon Laurel was shooing everyone out, assuring Jen they'd all be back tomorrow.

Ty didn't budge.

When her family was gone, she snuggled into him, ready for a nice long sleep.

"They'll make you leave," she murmured into his chest.

Ty only held on tighter. "Like hell, darling."

Epilogue

Ty cursed the crutch that had been a part of his life for too many months now. The surgery had been successful, but healing was annoying.

"You're pushing yourself too hard," Jen insisted as they walked across a stretch of rocky land at the edge of Carson property.

They'd been staying out at the Carson Ranch, where there weren't as many stairs to navigate as there were at his apartment above Rightful Claim and hers above the store.

Still, he was antsy to have a space of his own, to be done with healing and get on with living.

So, they'd start living. "What do you think?" he asked, waving a hand to encompass the stretch of field in front of them, the mountains sparkling in the blue-sky distance.

She smiled up at him, confusion written in her expression. She was the most beautiful woman he'd ever known, and she was all his. His faults and errors were no longer the black marks that held down his soul. Because in Jen he always had a place to find his salvation, and love.

"It's a pretty view," she offered.

"How'd you like a kitchen window looking out over that view?"

The confusion left her features, and something else he couldn't quite name replaced it. A certainty—the sure sign of a Jen Delaney plan in the works.

He found he quite liked going along with Jen Delaney's plans.

"I don't think I'd like it, I think I'd love it. But before you go getting ideas, there's one thing you're going to have to do first."

He dug around in his pocket, pulled out the velvet box and popped it open. Pleased that he'd managed to surprise her, he pulled the ring out and held it in the light so it sparkled. "This what you had in mind?"

She nodded wordlessly, tears already falling over her cheeks. He wiped one away, then took her hand.

"So, what do you say, Jen Delaney. Ready to promise your life to a Carson?"

"I always have been," she whispered, grinning at him, urging him to put the ring on her finger.

He slid it on easily, but kept her hand in his. "Anything else before we break ground?"

She took a deep, shaky breath. "I want lots of babies," she said, and though her voice wavered, her smile didn't. "Babies and forever. That should do it."

"We can start working on the babies thing right now if you're up to it."

She laughed, the sound carrying on the wind as it filled up his soul, because that was what his second chance with Jen had done—filled the empty places inside him, washed away the guilt he'd carried for so long.

Love and trust were that powerful, and he'd never let himself forget it.

He kissed her hands, looked into her eyes, and gave her the one thing he knew she'd never expect. The words. "I love you. I can't remember a time I didn't. I don't want to ever remember a time I didn't."

More tears spilled over, and she lightly wrapped her arms around his neck, careful not to move him so he had to put undue pressure on his foot. "I love you with everything I am," she whispered. "I always will. We can survive anything, so we will."

"Yeah, we will."

Always.

* * * * *

Don't miss the next book in Nicole Helm's
Carsons & Delaneys:
Battle Tested miniseries,
available July 2019
wherever Harlequin Intrigue books
and ebooks are sold.